And I
Held Her

Sheila Magee

12/9/ 2023

And I
Held Her

SHEILA MAGEE

And I Held Her
Copyright © 2023 Sheila Magee

Printed in the United States of America.

ISBN: 979-8-218-30383-9

Book Design by: Maureen Cutajar
Cover Design by: Jeff Crosby

Publisher: Taylor Publishing Group

ACKNOWLEDGEMENTS

I would like to acknowledge and thank four women who were my biggest cheerleaders throughout my journey of writing this book.

Cheryl King-Daniel – Thank you for being there for me in the beginning, when the book was mostly a figment of my imagination. You encouraged me by your eagerness for more, and by your love for the main characters.

Katelyn Jenkins – You spent your birthday weekend at the beach, reading the first few chapters of my book. Your excitement and encouragement impelled me to keep pushing, full speed ahead.

Monica Dudley – You loved the characters so much; you had arguments with them (out loud) each time you read parts of story. We had many conversations while I was writing, and your excitement about Daniel and Nicole pushed me to go further. My biggest thanks to you is telling me about the similarities between Nicole and me, which was something I didn't realize. Learning that in the middle of writing the story inspired me to dig deeper into the character and make her better than I could ever imagine her to be.

Zelda Magee – Thank you for the weekly talks, laughs, and your feedback about the characters in the book. They became so real to you; it was like they were your best friends. I know you fell in love with Daniel, and your comments helped me make him bigger and better than ever.

$\heartsuit$

Chapter 1

Nicole and I met five years ago at a fundraiser. I was immediately captivated by her million-dollar smile. She was easy to talk to and seemed to engage with everyone present. As the night came to an end, I offered to walk her to her car. She thanked me and smiled before turning to get into her car. On second look, I noticed the pain in her eyes. It was easily recognizable because it mirrored the pain in my own eyes. I was recently divorced, and later learned she had been divorced for three months. I was dealing with far too much to attempt a relationship with anyone, and I sensed she felt the same way. A few months later, I heard she was moving to Atlanta, Georgia. I had mixed emotions. Part of me wanted to rush forward and ask her out. The sensible part of me knew I needed to work on myself and my raw emotions.

I started working on myself, mentally, physically, and emotionally. Jogging became almost a daily thing for me.

It helped me in ways I never knew possible. It was now over five years since my divorce. Except for an occasional dinner out, I still wasn't dating. I'm not sure why I wasn't ready to take that step, and I wasn't going to dwell on it either. I was enjoying my run, and the beautiful weather, when I thought I heard someone call my name. I looked around, and, not seeing anyone I knew, continued running. A few moments later, I heard my name again. I looked around. Then, I saw her – Nicole – running towards me. I never knew she was also a runner.

"Daniel, I was hoping that was you, otherwise I would've made a complete fool of myself!" she casually laughed at herself.

She gave me that million-dollar smile. I was suddenly out of breath, which I attributed to the speed at which I had been running. "Nicole," I sputtered out, "I thought you had moved to Atlanta."

"I did, but decided I really missed North Carolina. I moved back here last week. This is my first day running. Boy, did I miss the beautiful parks here," she shared as she had a nostalgic reflection.

She was chattering easily, while my tongue seemed to be stuck to the roof of my mouth. Thankfully, she didn't notice that I was suddenly silent. She started running, so I ran along beside her. We ran three miles without talking, but I was aware of her presence.

All sorts of thoughts were running through my mind. I wanted to ask her out but wasn't quite sure what to say. I didn't understand what was happening to me. I'm a 64-year-old man, why was I suddenly feeling like a mushy

15-year-old? One thing I was sure of was that I didn't want to let another five years go by without seeing her again.

As we got close to the park entrance, I began to slow down. My heart was racing, and my legs were getting tired. I was also hungry and really didn't want to eat alone. We slowly made it to the parking lot, and I turned to her.

"I have two questions to ask you," I boldly stated.

Her right eyebrow arched upwards as she nodded for me to go ahead.

"When you yelled my name, how did you know it was me?" She had a look of relief. What did she think I was going to ask her?

"As I was walking into the park, I heard a guy call your name. I'm not sure why I looked your way, but when I did, I noticed your smile as the two of you shook hands and hugged each other. It was then that I noticed your dimples, which, by the way, was the first thing I ever noticed about you. I started a slow run, hoping that was really you, and gathering the nerve to say hello," she shyly stated.

"Oh, yeah, that was my friend Joe, and his wife Elaine. They got married a few months ago and Joe has been Missing in Action (MIA) since then. I'm glad you called my name; this has been an enjoyable and challenging run. Thank you for that."

Nicole cut me off abruptly, asking, "What's the second question?"

"Huh?" I gulped.

"You said you had two questions," she responded, pragmatically.

I really liked her directness; it was a breath of fresh air.

"Would you like to have lunch with me? That run has me starving," I said, while hoping I didn't appear to be begging.

She hesitated, and I felt she was trying to find a way to let me down easily. "I would love to, but I have to do it another day. The movers are delivering my furniture this afternoon, and I need to get ready for them. I probably won't be back to the park until next week."

"Here's my number, in case you need help. I'm handy with a hammer," I said, knowing I was flirting, and hoping it was working.

She smiled and gave me her number as well. We went in opposite directions in the parking lot. After a few steps, I accidentally dropped my keys. As I bent down to pick them up, I turned around to look at her. It seems she had accidentally dropped her keys too, because she was kneeling and looking in my direction. She smiled, and we waved goodbye once more. As I got into the car, the song "Brick House," by the Commodores was going through my head.

Chapter 2

Seeing Daniel again caught me totally off guard. The sensible side of me was saying, "slow down, Nicole", while another side of me, which I didn't recognize, and seemed to have little control over, was egging me on.

Whew, I don't remember him being so good looking! Every time he looked at me, those dimples turned me to mush. What is wrong with me? And why was I talking so much? I couldn't stop jabbering. It was nice of him to be so calm and quiet while I talked endlessly. Was I flirting with him?

Thank goodness, my sensible side kicked in and asked for a rain check for lunch. It won't take a week to get settled in my new house, but I need the time to get my mind together. I noticed he wasn't wearing a ring, but I don't know anything about what his life is like now. Let's just see if he calls!

I slowly walked toward my car, and knew I had to have one last glance at him, so I dropped my keys. I bent down to retrieve them and turned in his direction. To my surprise, he was kneeling, and looking in my direction. For seconds, we seemed suspended in time. The new, traitorous side of me kept trying to push me toward him, while my sensible side allowed me to stand gracefully and head to my car. I sat in the car for a few minutes, pretending to drink water, but I was really trying to lower my racing heart rate, and regain control. At that moment, both sides of me were collaborating, and I was hoping that I would see him again, the sooner, the better.

As I backed out of the parking space, the song, "Beautiful Morning," by the Rascals, ran through my mind.

Chapter 3

I wasn't sure if I should call Nicole that night or wait a few days. The voice in my head kept saying, "Daniel, take a leap of faith, what do you have to lose?" I knew I needed to stop overthinking everything and make a decision. If I was wrong, oh well!

I did call her, and a few days later, I went over to help her put up her curtain rods and hang pictures on the walls. I noticed she kept looking at me as I worked. I smiled to myself and was thankful that I made the right move.

For three months, we laughed, enjoyed each other's company, and had some delicious meals together. She was an excellent cook, and I discovered I was a pretty good cook too. I sent her a mushy text every night, and she returned the favor the next morning. We stayed away from talking about our exes, but both knew the time would come when we would talk about them. For now, we were happy, and didn't want our pasts to blemish what we were working on together.

We ran several times a week, all the while challenging each other to go further and faster. Her competitive nature was wearing off on me. I was in the best shape I've ever been in, and she was looking very hot! Of course, I thought that from the first day.

Everything seemed to be going quite well, until one day when I called her, she didn't answer. I waited a few hours to send her a text, and still no response. I was getting worried, so I hopped in the car and went to her house. I rang the doorbell three times before she finally answered the door. She opened the door wide enough for me to walk in. She stood in the middle of the living room with her arms folded tightly across her chest. The expression on her face was one I'd never seen before. Neither of us spoke, we just kept looking at each other. My mind was racing as I tried to think what I did to make her act this way.

Finally, I calmly said, "When we started dating exclusively, I promised I would not let a day go by without talking with you. No matter what we're going through, I promised to end the day on a good note."

She just glared at me.

I pointed to my chest and said, "I'm going to keep my promise."

She still glared!

I was at a loss. I didn't have a clue what was going on, let alone how to fix it. My heart was pounding, and I couldn't think of what to do next. I took a step toward her, pulled her in my arms, and I held her. The surprise of my action caused her to drop her tightly folded arms. Her arms hung stiffly by her side. I still held her. We stood that way for what seemed like an eternity, but I wasn't going to let go. Finally, I felt a slight motion, and her arms wrapped around my waist. I still held her. After a few moments, I pulled back, and lifted her chin to get a look at her beautiful face. She looked up at me, and her eyes looked glassy, as if she was going to cry. I was racking my brain trying to figure out what I had done to make her look that way. At that moment, I realized I was madly in love with her. I also realized the look on her face wasn't anger, she was hurt. I never wanted to be the one to make her look that way. I needed to fix this. Without her input, I didn't know where to begin. I pulled her toward me, and I held her.

After a few minutes, I noticed my shirt was getting wet. She was crying! I think if it was noisy, dramatic tears, I could handle it better. Instead, she was silent, and the tears flowed. And I held her, fighting my own emotions.

After a while, she stopped crying, and began to hold me tighter. I was still at a loss, as I reached down to wipe her tears. My heart seemed to swell when she looked at me with so much emotion. I looked her in the eyes and told her I loved her. She smiled, and I leaned in further to kiss her. What was going to be a smack on the lips ended up being a passionate kiss. She kissed me back and we clung to each other. Both of us were breathing heavily. And I held her!

"Honey, let's sit down and talk. Please tell me why you're so upset," I reassured Nicole, hoping it would help her open up.

She swallowed hard, and said," I met Carolyn Jackson."

The mention of my ex-wife made me feel sick. We had not crossed paths in at least three years. As hard as it was, I decided to stay calm and let her get it all out.

"She has a good friend named Cathy Mason," Nicole said.

"Ooookay," I responded, wondering where this was going.

"Cathy is my neighbor down the street. She's been trying to get me to go out to lunch with her and her friends for the last month. I've always turned her down, mainly because I don't think I like her very much. Anyway, I was out watering my roses this morning when she and Carolyn walked up my driveway. I didn't realize who she was until Cathy told me that Carolyn was getting a divorce from her husband. I said I was sorry, and Carolyn said, no worries, she was going back to her ex, Daniel. My heart sank, because I then realized who she was, and that she was talking about you. I noticed they were both looking at me for a reaction, and at that exact moment, you called. I looked at the phone, smiled, and very politely excused myself," Nicole said through the emotional rollercoaster that she was feeling inside.

"It sounds like my timing was good, but why didn't you answer my call?" I asked with a puzzled look on my face.

"I was stunned and needed a moment. I wanted to hit something and didn't want it to be you. I also had a feeling how you would react and didn't want to risk you getting arrested. I needed time to get myself together before talking with you about it. When you texted me, I just wasn't ready to talk. "I'm sorry I worried you, but I was too emotional," Nicole stated matter-of-factly.

I reached out, held her hands and asserted, "I know what you're thinking, and I don't want you to confront her. My way of handling it is to not give her the attention she wants. I know she will think of another way to get to us, and hopefully, we'll be better prepared the next time."

As I exhaled, and tried to contain my emotions, she stood up, pulling me with her. She held my hand and started walking toward the bedroom. She shut the door and started to unbutton my shirt. I usually like to be the one to initiate this step, especially since it was our first time. I decided to let go of my male ego and follow her lead. After undressing me, she slowly began taking off her own clothes. She had an incredible body!

We got into bed and started kissing. I was having a hard time restraining myself. I looked into her eyes. She smiled, and my heart felt full.

I held her hands, and said, "I hope you know you're the only one for me. I will never cheat on you. If we ever get to a point where things aren't working, please, let's talk about it. I love you."

She smiled and gave me a deep kiss. I pleasured her until she looked spent. Now it was my turn!

What started out slow and easy quickly heated up. I was completely out of control. I made love to her until we both were worn out. I kissed her again, and then, I held her. I never wanted to let go of this moment. As I was falling asleep, I thought of an old song by Barry White, called "What Am I Gonna Do With You?" The lyrics seemed to fit this moment perfectly. I held her tightly and we both fell into a deep sleep.

Chapter 4

Meeting Carolyn was very difficult for me. Although I know Daniel is not interested in her, it still hurt to hear her say she was going back to him. I've never been a person who engaged in drama of any kind, especially in relationships. There was a time when I would have walked away from this type of nonsense without a second thought, and never looked back. This time was different, and it triggered emotions in me that I didn't understand. I knew it wasn't jealousy, but whatever it was made me see red. Part of me wanted to smack her so hard it would make her wig fly across the driveway. I also kept thinking she looked familiar, but I can't imagine the two of us traveling in the same circles. It took a while for the logical part of me to kick in and realize she and her friend Cathy were having their dramatic moment at my expense. I don't understand why I didn't recognize it immediately.

SHEILA MAGEE

When Daniel came over, I was in quite a state. It took everything I had in me to open the door and let him in. I was still processing my emotions and didn't know what to say to him. I am so thankful for his calm spirit, and his patience. Years of unshed tears, which I had stored inside of me were released, and I couldn't control my emotions. The tears kept flowing, and his shirt became wet with the overflow. He held me and let me cry until I got it all out. When he told me he loved me, I almost melted in his arms. I always knew he cared, even though we both had skirted around the "L" word. It was at that moment that I understood the emotions I was having that day; I was in love with him, not just in love; madly, head over heels in love. I've known for a while that I was falling for him, but, until that moment, I didn't realize the intensity of my feelings.

When we made love, I knew for sure, that I was the center of his world. I felt loved and blessed! On top of all his wonderful traits, he had a HOT body!

As I drifted off to sleep, the words to "At Last," a song by Etta James played over and over in my mind. My love has come along, and I am so happy. Just as he does for me, I will think of ways to keep him happy and to keep our love special. My heart is full. I'm soooo much in love!

Chapter 5

*E*laine and I were beginning to spend a lot of time together. We decided to celebrate our new friendship by pampering ourselves. We started the day with a manicure, pedicure, and massage. I don't think I've ever been so relaxed.

"So, Elaine," I said, "What's next?"

"Shopping, of course," she responded, with an astonished look on her face.

"I'm not much of a shopper. I usually make a list, buy what I need, and go home."

"Well, Nicole, we'll have to change that. Don't worry, I'll go easy on you this first time. Joe and I are having a date night on Saturday, and I need a new dress. I promise, we'll just go to one store, then we can have lunch."

Shopping was not as bad as I've always made it out to be. I've heard it is called retail therapy, and I'm sure I probably won't be using it in that way. I found two beautiful dresses and was finished. Thankfully, Elaine found what she wanted, and we headed to lunch.

As we waited for our food, we started talking about the upcoming Christmas season. I asked Elaine what their plans were for the holiday.

"Joe and I decided we would go to Jamaica for two weeks. We didn't have a honeymoon, so this will be perfect," she stated, with a gleam in her eyes.

"That is awesome! Jamaica is on my bucket list. I can't wait to hear all about it when you return, Elaine. Daniel and I are volunteering with the Food Bank. We adopted three families, and will meet with them for dinner, fun, and a big surprise --- Santa Daniel. He's been practicing in the mirror the last few days. I'm looking forward to it."

"That is sooo cute," she said, with a girlish giggle.

"I'll have to text you and Joe some pictures. This is our first Christmas together, and I wanted to do something different. I asked that we exchange gifts on New Years Eve, and that the gifts needed to be non-monetary," I responded matching her excitement.

"That sounds like a great idea, Nicole, I may copy it,"

"Please, feel free to copy it. I think the gift idea will take a little pressure off us both."

"Did you have a hard time getting Daniel to agree to it?" Elaine questioned.

"In the beginning I did, but I think he's warming up to the idea. We have each other, and that is priceless. Besides, I get more excited about my birthday than I get about Christmas. I'm like a giddy five-year-old. I've been talking about it since October, which I call my half birthday. Daniel asked what I wanted, but I'll leave that up to him. He's good at surprising me, and I can't wait to see what he plans."

At that moment, our food arrived, and we dived into it. We decided we would also have dessert and ordered strawberry cheesecake.

The meal was delicious. I was enjoying our time together and was eager to learn more about her.

"So, how did you and Joe meet," I asked. Elaine grinned as she shared their story with me.

"I was a radiology technology instructor at the community college. One of my students was having her first solo weekend rotation. I decided I would pop in and check on her. She said she was bored to tears, so we started to practice doing x-rays on different body parts. There was a loud knock on the door, and when I answered, Joe and Daniel were standing there. It seems they were playing basketball, like wannabe NBA players, with a bunch of teenagers. Joe tripped and fell but continued playing. By the end of their game, his ankle was swelling and turning colors. I took the x-rays, and while my student was developing the film, the three of us chatted. He and Daniel have been friends since college freshman year. They met on a double date with twin sisters. It didn't work out with the sisters, but the two of them remained friends."

"Elaine, that's so cute!" I exclaimed.

"Yeah, except they keep forgetting they aren't college students anymore. I don't know what made them think they could beat a bunch of teenagers. It turned out Joe had a very bad sprain, luckily no broken bones," Elaine paused as the waitress brought the cheesecake to our table. We nodded at each other in agreeance because it was delicious. Elaine washed it down with her beverage and continued with the story.

"The next week, I received a bouquet of flowers at work. There was a note saying, *'Since you've seen my insides, would you have dinner with me?'* I thought it was corny, but cute, so, I said yes. We've been inseparable since then. We dated for three years before deciding to get married. Joe had been a widower for 10 years, and I had been divorced about the same amount of time,"

"What a great story! You seem perfect for each other," I gushed.

"So do you and Daniel" Elaine interjected, "I've never seen him so happy. I know he teases Joe about being MIA, but I've also heard Joe teasing him about eating salads and turkey burgers since he met you and enjoying them. He won't even eat steak anymore,"

We both had a good laugh as we headed to our cars. It had been an enjoyable day, and the beginning of a great friendship.

Chapter 6

Nicole and I made it through a wonderful Christmas holiday. I'm so happy she encouraged me to volunteer with her at the Food Bank. It felt good to be helping others. I'm not bragging, but I think I made a pretty good Santa.

Finally, it was New Years Eve. I was excited about ringing in a New Year with her, and about our gift exchange. At first, I thought her idea of exchanging gifts on New Years Eve instead of Christmas was a little crazy. Then she added the part about the gift being non-monetary. She didn't say I couldn't get help, so that's what I did!

The day was unusually warm, so we decided to grill and eat on the deck. I needed to get her out of the house for a bit to get my surprise in place, so I accidentally dropped the glass bottle of salad dressing. I begged her to run to the store to get some more. I also added a few other things so she wouldn't get suspicious. She looked at me like I had lost my mind, but she didn't complain. When she returned 30 minutes later, I was ready.

"Nicole, are you getting excited about your birthday, "I asked.

"My birthday isn't for four more months," she responded, acting surprised that I didn't know that.

"I know, but you told me you're like a five-year-old in the months leading up to your birthday. I'm sure you're counting the days. Is it 80, or 85 days until the big day?"

"Actually, it's 97," she sighed, while rolling her eyes.

"Ahhh, but you're not really counting, are you? What would you like to do for your birthday?"

" I don't know yet," Nicole quickly responded.

We made it through dinner, washed dishes together, and listened to oldies music while cuddling on the couch.

"Are you ready for our gift exchange," I asked. I knew I was probably the one acting like a giddy five-year-old, but I didn't care at that moment.

"Sure, let's do it," she said.

"Ladies first," I proclaimed.

"No, you go ahead," she stated, with an amused look on her face.

"I need to put this blindfold over your eyes for just a moment while I get everything set up. Please don't peek." I gently covered her eyes.

She sat on the sofa with her back to the hallway, as I slid a box across the floor. I took her hand and led her towards the dining room area. When I removed the blindfold, she looked down at a big cardboard box.

"Daniel, remember, non-monetary," she said.

"Honey, please don't judge, come closer," I said with excitement while guiding her.

I lifted the box, and there was a little house sitting underneath. The outside was made of a material which resembled brick. I took her hand and we both sat on the floor. I was enjoying her shocked look. The front door had a little heart with our names on it. I opened the door and pointed to a miniature picture of us on one of the walls. Another wall had a sign that said, *"The house that Daniel built"*. There was even an area with fake plants. It looked so much like a real home. Even the chimney was made to look like smoke was coming out of it.

"Wow, this is awesome," she gushed, with her mouth open in astonishment.

"I hope you like it. I designed it, all the materials were donations from my construction friends, and my students helped me put it together. I gave them extra credit towards their engineering project for the semester."

Nicole was close to tears. After helping her stand up, I kissed her, pulled her close to my body, and I held her.

"By the way, honey, the house has symbolism. The engineering side of me wants you to know there is a solid foundation, just like our love for each other. Nothing, or nobody can destroy it. The man in me wants you to notice it's a brick house, which is what I think of you," I confidently remarked.

That made us both smile.

We kissed again, and Nicole looked at me with so much love in her eyes. I was on cloud nine. She placed both hands over the left side of her chest. When she pulled her hands away, she held them together, as if she were holding something. She looked up at me and said, "Daniel, I'm giving you the most vulnerable, and most guarded part of me; I'm giving you my heart. I know you will take good care of it."

She put her hands on my chest, and I placed my hands over hers, as if we were merging our hearts together. We took a bubble bath together – her idea – then laid in bed talking. It was 11 pm, well past both of our bedtimes. We were determined to stay awake and welcome the New Year.

"Honey, thank you for a wonderful year. I really look forward to what the future holds for us. I love your gift exchange idea; we will have to make that a tradition. Since we're being nontraditional, I have two songs I want to play for you – one to end this year, and the other to begin the new year," I said, with a smile.

I had recorded "Oh What a Night," by the Dells. As the song played, we kissed, then made love, slow and easy. I was enjoying this moment with the love of my life.

"Daniel, I love the song, the house, and I especially love the symbolism. You did a great job," Nicole smiled brightly.

One thing led to another, and before we knew it, the time was 11:55. "Honey, thank you for your heart. I will love you and cherish you forever. Your heart will always have a place right next to mine, close enough so that our hearts will always be touching. Now, here's my New Year song for us."

As Al Green began singing "Let's Stay Together", I reached for her hand. At the stroke of midnight, we were holding each other tightly, as we rang in the New Year our way!

Chapter 7

Upon waking, I rolled over to hug Nicole, and found her side of the bed empty. Before I could wonder where she was, I smelled breakfast cooking. I ran into the bathroom to clean up a bit, and as I walked down the hall, I heard her singing. I stood by the kitchen door and watched her. She was holding a spoon in her hand, as if it were a microphone. She began singing the words, "I love you for so many reasons", in a loud tone. She was dancing around as she sang. I couldn't resist smiling because I knew she was talking about me. I walked into the kitchen and began dancing with her.

"Honey, what are you singing," I asked, as I gave her a kiss.

She smiled and said, "It's a song called 'I Love You for All Seasons,' by a group called The Fuzz."

She stopped singing, and we sat down to eat. I didn't realize how hungry I was, as I began to dig in. She's a morning person, but this morning she seemed more bubbly than usual. I just kept eating; I would explore that later. I noticed she was staring at me as I took my last bite.

"Are you ok?" I asked.

"I'm more than ok, I'm in love with the most wonderful man on earth. I just feel like singing. Thank you for a wonderful evening, and for always being by my side. Loving you is the highlight of my day," she responded, with a big grin on her face.

I couldn't stop smiling. She made a comment about my dimples, and I smiled even more.

"So, I guess we're not going out for a run," I said, trying to look shocked.

"Ah, noooo!" She was quite emphatic about that.

"So, what are we going to do for exercise?" I asked.

She rolled her eyes, and I thought I heard her mutter something about men, under her breath. She took my hand and led me down the hall. We were barely in the bedroom before she began removing my clothes. She did a slow strip tease as she removed her own clothes. I loved this sexy side of her, but I acted like I didn't know what was going on. She kept kissing me, and we got into bed. She made love to me in a way I had never been loved. I'm not sure where she got so much energy, as it seemed like this was never going to end. I wasn't complaining, just wanted to reciprocate before my energy ran out. She gave me the biggest smile as she shook her head. I realized this was her show, so I gave in, and let her have her way with me. And she did, over, and over again. "Whew!"

If I smoked, I would need a cigarette at this moment. I pulled her in my arms, and we both fell asleep.

When we woke up, I noticed I had a text from Joe. He and Elaine returned to town yesterday and were inviting us to dinner tonight. I knew Nicole and I wouldn't make it too far from the bedroom today, so I responded and told him tomorrow would be better.

We took a long shower together, then returned to bed. For some reason, we couldn't keep our hands off each other. "Honey, I decided to take you on a trip for your birthday," I said, as I hugged her.

Her eyes grew large as she asked where we were going.

"It's a surprise," I responded.

"I need to know what to pack," Nicole probed more.

I knew where she was going with this, and I wasn't giving in.

"The only hint I'm giving you is that we are leaving three days before your birthday and staying for a week." I knew I had a smirk on my face as I responded.

"So, you're going to torture me for the next four months?" she asked.

"For 97 days, yeah! I will tell you where we're going the day before we leave. By the way, honey, I know there's a side of you that needs to research and investigate everything. Let that side rest for now. Nicole, I want this to be a birthday you'll never forget. Please be patient and enjoy the time leading to your big day."

She looked at me with disbelief as I said, "One more thing, honey, you are quite charming, and sometimes I have a hard time resisting you. Your charm will not work on me this time."

Her mouth dropped open, and before she could say anything, I kissed her. I pulled her close to me, and this time, I had my way with her!

$\heartsuit$

Chapter 8

Nicole and Elaine were volunteering at the Food Bank, so Joe and I ran alone. The timing was perfect. I told him a little about the vacation I planned for Nicole's birthday. I needed his help, plus, I wanted Elaine to be prepared in case Nicole started asking questions.

The four of us had dinner together that night and Nicole was very quiet. Elaine showed what seemed like a zillion pictures of their trip to Jamaica. It truly was a beautiful country, and I could tell Nicole was impressed. Elaine had told me Jamaica was on Nicole's bucket list, and that information really helped. She also managed to find out that Nicole had a current passport.

The people at the Food Bank were keeping her busy, which helped the time go by faster. I was impressed at how well she was taking the lack of information about my surprise. Thankfully, she had stopped asking questions. I almost felt sorry for her, but not really. I knew she would be happy in the end.

It was April at last. I must admit, I was relieved to finally stop withholding information. I took Nicole to dinner, and when we got back to the car, I handed her an envelope. Inside was a note which said "Happy birthday month. Please come with me and explore Jamaica."

The grin on her face was so cute. I love seeing the giddy five-year-old in her come out. She didn't know this was just the beginning. I had big plans for the next few days.

She was bubbling over with excitement as our plane landed in Jamaica. We picked up our bags, and I started searching for the Uber driver. Finally, I saw him holding a sign with my name on it. On the way to our Airbnb, she was asking the driver a million questions about the area. I swear, that woman can get anyone to talk.

"Look honey," I said, as we pulled into the driveway.

"Wow, this house is beautiful!" Nicole screamed out.

I held her hand as I carried the bags inside, "Let's leave the bags by the door and explore the house."

When we got to the kitchen door, I backed away and let her go in first. The room was filled with birthday balloons.

Her eyes were as big as saucers as she asked, "How did they know it was my birthday?"

I just smiled. She was so happy that she didn't notice I wasn't talking. I hugged her and she reached up and planted a big kiss on my lips.

"Let's change clothes and explore a bit," I said.

We took a walk around the area, then stopped at a cute restaurant for dinner. The food was delicious. We headed back to our temporary home, and she babbled all the way.

We got home and played in the hot tub. Soon it was bedtime.

"Daniel, this is the best birthday I ever had. Thank you so much!" Nicole was so grateful she repeated herself, "Thank you so much!"

I smiled and pulled her closer to me, "I'm so glad you're enjoying yourself."

We kissed, and before I knew it, we were sprawled across the bed making love. The next morning, we had a quick three-mile run, then came home to shower and eat breakfast. We were listening to music and relaxing when the doorbell rang. We looked at each other, and I opened the door to two young ladies. I had a moment with them, then walked outside to their van. When we came back, I told Nicole they were here to give us a couples massage. I helped them set up their equipment in the living room.

I had never had a massage before and had no idea how relaxing they could be. This is something we will have to do more often when we return home. After saying goodbye to the young ladies, I turned the music on, and we fell asleep cuddled in each other's arms. Later, we made a salad for dinner, and relaxed some more. We went to bed early. Tomorrow was the big day, and I needed all my energy.

I woke early and went to the kitchen to begin my surprise. When I returned to the bedroom, I saw Nicole gazing out of the window. I cleared my throat to get her attention, and she turned in my direction, with a big smile. I began singing Happy Birthday to her. I held a cupcake in my hand and instructed her to blow out the candle and make a wish.

"Do you mind me asking what your wish was," I inquired.

She smiled and said, "I couldn't think of anything more to wish for, so my wish was that we will always be as happy as we are at this moment."

"Your wish is my command," I said, as I leaned forward to kiss her.

We went to the kitchen to eat. I was feeling nervous and a bit antsy, and, luckily, Nicole didn't appear to notice. She wanted to linger over breakfast, but I told her we needed to hurry, as I had scheduled a four-hour River Falls Party Cruise. The cruise was far more than we could ever have imagined. The views were beautiful, the food was outstanding, and the people were so nice. I was finally able to breathe a sigh of relief when I saw how much she was enjoying herself.

Later that evening, we sat around holding hands, hugging, and kissing. I asked her to dance with me. Although there was no music playing, we still danced and held each other closely. I couldn't stop gazing into her eyes.

"Honey, I've searched for a while for the perfect song to say exactly how I feel about you, and how I feel about us. I finally found it. It's a song by John Legend, called "All of Me." Please listen to the words," I said, with a mushy grin on my face.

The first words of the song were, "What would I do without your smart mouth"? I know I had a smirk on my face as the song continued.

The song ended, yet we still clung to each other. "Honey, all of me really does love all of you. Let's have a seat and relax," I said.

"Nicole, a few months ago, you gave me your heart. I accepted it, and it will forever be intertwined with mine.

I got down on one knee, as I continued, "Now I'm asking you to accept my heart, all my love, and my name. Will you marry me?"

She began to cry when I took the ring out of my pocket and placed it on her finger.

"I'm going to take your reaction as a Yes," I said, trying to lighten the mood.

"Yes! Yes! yes! Daniel, I'm the luckiest woman on earth. I'm looking forward to spending the rest of my life with you. Hmmm, Nicole Washington, I love the way that sounds."

Chapter 9

We awoke to the relaxing sound of rain pounding against the windows. This would be a perfect day to stay home and chill out. The last few days have been exciting but draining. I woke several times during the night to find Nicole gazing at the ring on her finger. I can't wait to make her my wife. We showered together, then she went to cook breakfast. I just sat in the kitchen and watched her. After breakfast, I washed dishes while she vacuumed the downstairs.

"Honey, have you been enjoying Jamaica," I asked.

"Yes, I love it! You made the trip and my birthday special. Thank you so much."

"Would you like to come back again, and stay in a different neighborhood," I asked.

"I would love to come back. We don't need to explore other neighborhoods. This is perfect. I love this house, Daniel."

I smiled and took her hand as I said, "Honey, I have one more surprise for you."

"Another birthday surprise," she asked, with a little girl grin on her face.

"Actually, it was going to be a Christmas surprise, but you changed all of the rules, so I decided to wait until the right time. We can come back any time you want because I own this house."

She had a shocked look on her face, so I decided not to delay telling her the whole story. I proceeded with the story, "Several years ago, the engineering firm I worked with was doing a project in this area. The neighborhood was complete, and most of the homes had been sold. This house was the model. One of the builders told me they were going to sell this one, and if I was interested, I had first dibs. The timing was perfect, as this was my last assignment with my company. I planned to turn in my hard hat and retire. I was going to work three more months, travel a bit, then begin a new career as a professor at the university from which I graduated. We discussed all the details, and I knew buying the house would be the perfect surprise for Carolyn. I told him I wanted to talk it over with my wife, and he said that was fine, but he needed an answer within seven days. I was scheduled to fly home the next day, but I called to see if I could get a flight out that evening instead. Thankfully, they had a seat, so I finished my workday and went to the airport."

I paused before continuing, "After boarding, I sent a text to Carolyn to tell her I had a big surprise for her. She texted back that she couldn't wait. I was composing another text to tell her I was coming home that night when the captain instructed us to turn off our electronic devices for take-off. It had been a long day, so I sat back to relax, and fell asleep. It was late when I got in town, so I decided to take an Uber instead of asking her to pick me up."

Noticing a questionable look upon Nicole's face as one eyebrow was raised, I further shared, "I had been gone for a week and was so happy to be home again. I figured she would be sleeping, so I tried to be as quiet as possible. I ran up the stairs, and as I approached the bedroom door, I heard moaning. I pushed open the door, only to find Carolyn and some guy having a good time, in my bed! My first instinct was to kick his ass, so I went with that feeling. I grabbed him, and punched him, twice. I was going for the third time when I heard Carolyn yelling at me to stop. Her voice brought me back to my senses. The little punk grabbed his clothes and ran out of the room."

Nicole squeezed my hand as I continued telling my story, "Carolyn and I stood glaring at each other". I calmly said, "I would never lay a hand on a woman, but don't test me at this moment. She was used to me being very calm, but I know she realized I was very serious. I walked out of the room and went downstairs. Shortly after, she came downstairs with her suitcase and went out the front door."

I squeezed Nicole's hand and feeling her warmth calmed me from my traumatic memories, "The next day, I contacted a divorce attorney. After telling him what happened the night before, he told me he was going to check the police records to see if there was any pending assault charge attached to my name. There weren't any yet, so we decided to get the process started. Considering the circumstances, I wanted out of this marriage with as little debt to me as possible, and as quickly as possible. He predicted it could possibly be over within four months, six at the most. I had bought the house before Carolyn and I married, and I didn't want to split that with her either. I felt better after my meeting with him, and after leaving, I went to the hardware store to get new locks for the doors. I also updated the alarm system and cameras."

Feeling more at ease I continued my story, "I knew Joe had worked in the ER the night before, so I waited a few hours before calling to talk with him. He said it was perfect timing, he was about to put some steaks on the grill, and we could have dinner and catch up. I know he had a sweet tooth, so I picked up dessert. We sat down for our steak and potatoes meal, then went into the living room to watch a ball game. I began telling him what happened the night before. Halfway through my story, I noticed him staring at me. I asked what was wrong, and he said a man had come into the ER last night and had been beaten. He had a broken nose. I felt pretty sure that had to be the same guy. All I could think was he better be glad that was all that was broken. I didn't push Joe for more information because I knew he really couldn't talk about it."

Nicole snuggled closer to me, holding my hand, as I continued, "I have to give Joe most of the credit for helping me get my life back together. He asked me to go with him to his support group meeting the next evening. I wasn't a person who could sit around talking about my feelings, but I was sure he recognized something in me that I couldn't see at that moment. I promised to tag along but told him I would probably not do any talking. He was ok with that."

"When I got home, I looked over the videos from the old alarm system. I was glad I thought to download and save them before switching the system. I found several good pictures of the guy from last night. Thank goodness for technology. I went on social media and found his picture on several of Carolyn's sites. Now I had a name to go with the face. As I went further with my research, I didn't think I had to worry about him pressing assault charges, it seems he had a wife! It would be a bit hard, as well as foolish for him to tell the truth about his broken nose."

"Joe was a recent widower when he, a psychologist, and our Pastor, started the group by accident. They were just sitting around talking one evening and realized this was good for all of them. I know that's something you ladies learn early, but it takes us guys a while. The group has been going strong since then. The good thing is you don't feel like you're under a microscope, and there are guys from all age groups, with many different careers, and a variety of issues. It's a no judgement zone, which makes it easier to express yourself. I didn't talk the first night, but I sure learned a lot about myself."

Nicole further investigated, "Really, like what?"

"Well, I got home and thought about what some of

the guys talked about. I even talked out loud to myself, sort of like role playing. I decided if I was going to work through this, I needed to stop dwelling on what Carolyn had done to me and our marriage and ask myself what I didn't do along the way to prevent this. I wasn't letting her off the hook by any means, but I realized this was about my survival and healing. I needed to work on me at that moment. My emotions were all over the place, and I wasn't used to that. I also learned forgiveness is sometimes a solo thing. Holding on to bad feelings for the other person doesn't help at all. After the second meeting, I was able to let her come to the house and get her things. It was awkward but I made it through."

"At the third meeting, I finally talked about my feelings, thoughts, and emotions. It was surprisingly helpful. When we talked before the group the first time, we were encouraged to tell what we hoped to get out of the group meetings. At that moment, I knew I wanted to come out of this as a better man, rather than a bitter one. I went from never wanting to have a relationship again, to hoping I would get one more chance. I knew the next lady in my life would know she was loved and cared for. She would never have to wonder or look elsewhere to fulfill her needs. The group cheered, and I knew I was on the right track."

I noticed the intent look on Nicole's face and decided to pause for a moment. I leaned forward and gave her a hug before continuing my story.

"I continued the sessions faithfully for four months. Shortly after then, my divorce was final. I still attend the meetings sporadically, but more as an advisor and helper. The night I first met you at the fundraiser, I had just learned Carolyn was getting married to the guy I found her in bed with. He had also divorced his wife. At first, I felt like I had been kicked in the stomach. It hurt, but not as much as it would have had I not attended the support meetings."

"So, that's my story, and how I got to the place I am today." The rain has stopped, "Do you want to go out for lunch? When we come back, I'd like to hear your story," I prompted Nicole.

She hugged me, and at that moment I was so happy I had worked hard to give myself a second chance.

Chapter 10

knew it was time to tell my story. I've never been good at expressing my feelings, and I was a bit nervous. I glanced at Daniel, and seeing the loving look in his eyes, reassured me there was no need to worry. I began sharing.

"Charles and I were a power couple. He owned his own company, and I was an executive in the company I worked for. He was my biggest cheerleader, always encouraging me to climb as high as I wanted. He always told me the sky was the limit, so I had plenty of room for growth and success."

"One night he came home from an out- of -town business meeting and asked for a divorce. That was totally out of left field. I never saw that coming. I asked him to please sit down and talk with me. He started out with that age-old line about it's not you, it's me. I wanted to slap some sense into him, but I kept my cool. He started rambling, and his thoughts seemed to be all over the place. He told me I didn't have to worry; he was willing to give me a large settlement. At that moment, I knew something was up. I looked him square in the eyes, even though he was having a hard time looking at me. I told him to stop the bullshit and give me the real story. He couldn't hide his shock at my words. Finally, he told me he had been having an affair. That was bad enough, but then he continued to say she was 20 years younger, and pregnant. That part really hurt. I always wanted kids and he never did, so he said," I paused for a moment, as the painful memories hit me.

Daniel leaned in closer with a tighter embrace to let me know he cared. I continued to share, "It took me a moment to digest this news, and I was silent at first. I think he took that as some sort of positive sign for him. Little did he know he would not have been able to handle the thoughts that were going through my mind at that time. Next, he pulled out divorce papers and asked me to sign them. I threw the papers in his face and left the room."

"The next morning, he started up again, and I asked what the rush was. He said she wanted to get married before the baby was born. I was not going to sign anything and told him so. I would get my own attorney and do things properly. If he was in such a hurry to get rid of me, he was certainly going to pay. Forget being nice, or calm, I was mad as hell!!!" I threw my hands up in exasperation.

"I started the process with my attorney, who made sure I was compensated for what he called my pain and suffering. Initially, I didn't want material things from Charles, but I did want him to suffer. As time went on, I began to agree with my attorney, and felt Charles owed me, for what he was putting me through. After all, he had turned my life upside down. I asked him what prompted him to have an affair with another woman, and one so young. His response was, she needed him, I didn't." I shook my head in disbelief.

"The divorce went through, and I began the difficult job of healing. It seemed I would have good days when it felt like I was making a lot of progress, then I would have days when I felt like the rug was being pulled from under me. The night I met you at the fundraiser, I was having one of those days. A few hours before it started, I learned that Charles had become the father of a bouncing baby boy. That news really hurt."

Daniel pulled me closer to him, "That explains the pain I noticed in your eyes when I walked you to your car."

"I was going through a myriad of emotions that night. I knew I had to give the presentation for my company, and I didn't know which way was up. I finally looked in the mirror, and told myself to just do it, I could fall apart later," I shared while exhibiting the confidence that I had built up.

"Wow, from listening to your speech, I never would have known you were going through anything as bad as that. I remember admiring your poise and grace. I also thought you were very attractive," Daniel reassured me, but I knew he was stunned by the story. I continued telling him.

"Inside I was a boiling hot mess. A few months later the president of my company asked if I was willing to head a new branch in Atlanta. He said he wanted it to be started properly. I agreed to do it, on the condition that I would get it going the first four years, then give them six months to find a new leader. He agreed to those terms."

"So, moving to Atlanta was sort of an escape for me. I really didn't want to keep running into Charles and his girl toy, and baby. It turned out to be a positive move for me, but I really missed this area," I somberly stated.

"You were amazingly strong, I admire that. Now we can put our exes to bed, so to speak, and concentrate on the life we are building together. Did I tell you today how much I love you?" Daniel lovingly said, and that melted away the painful memories.

I smiled, and said "Yep, around the time you asked what you would do without my smart mouth."

That made us both laugh and helped to ease the necessary tension we had experienced that day. Now it was time to really enjoy our last few days in this paradise.

♡

Chapter 11

We sat on the runway waiting for takeoff. Nicole leaned on my shoulder to look out of the window and get a last glance at what she called her new favorite place. We agreed that this week had been amazing. We were looking forward to coming back. Once we were safely in the air, we fell asleep, waking just as we were landing at home.

Luckily, the airport wasn't too busy, and we were able to get our bags and head to the car in record time. It was good to be home.

I knew Nicole was ready to go home, change clothes, and relax, but I told her I needed to stop by my house first. She had only been to my house a few times. I didn't think she felt comfortable being there, so I never pushed it. I pulled into the garage and asked her to come in with me. I took her hand as we walked through the kitchen, headed for the living room. The room was filled with congratulations balloons. There was a bouquet of roses on the coffee table, with a card next to it.

"Daniel, this is so sweet! When did you have time to do all of this?" Nicole asked with glee.

"I can't take credit for this, let's read the card," I picked up the card and began to read. It was from Joe and Elaine:

> *Dear Nicole and Daniel, congratulations on your engagement. We are so happy for you. Nicole, we hope you had a great birthday. Thank you for texting the picture of your happy faces. You are perfect for each other, and we're so glad you have found the love you both deserve. Cheers to you both!*
>
> *PS: We know you'll probably be tired from your trip, so dinner is in the fridge. Enjoy! We would love to get together tomorrow night and see your glowing faces in person.*
>
> *Love, Elaine and Joe*

"That is so sweet! You didn't know about this?" Nicole blushed like a giddy five-year-old.

"Not really, they have the keys to the house, and I knew Joe was coming by to check on things today. I saw his car pull in the driveway on the security camera, but he parked in the garage, so I didn't see anything after that. He sent me a text and said Elaine had left something here for you. This was a nice surprise. Let's see what they left for dinner," I opened the fridge and pulled a large pan out. There was a dish of Elaine's homemade lasagna, with a note saying it was made with turkey, and not beef. That made us both laugh. She had also made a great-looking salad. On the counter, there was a bottle of sparkling grape juice, and two wine glasses. They were such romantics. We sent them a thank you text and sat down to eat.

We enjoyed our moment together. Now I know why Joe had been MIA since marrying Elaine. I made a mental note to not tease him about it anymore. We knew our lives and schedules would get back to normal in a few days, but for now, it felt good to be in a dream world of our own making.

"Honey, would you stay here with me tonight?" I asked.

She didn't answer right away, and I think I knew why. "I think I have an idea what's going through your pretty little head. Just to put your mind at ease, my bedroom furniture is not the same as what I had when I was married," I reassured her.

She slowly exhaled, and I felt I had nailed her concern.

"It's really creepy the way you seem to read my mind," Nicole smirked.

"Not reading your mind, I'm very in tuned to you, just as you are to me."

"That's one of the things I love the most about you, Daniel."

"One of the things? That must mean there are others. Please tell me more, "I said, giving her my best dimpled smile.

She turned to me while gazing into my eyes and said, "I love how you're so kind, and loving, and how you treat me like I'm the center of your universe. I love how you look up and smile when I enter the room. I love how you don't mind yielding and giving me control at times, but you also know how and when to take the control back without beating your chest and acting like a macho man. I love sitting and talking with you about everything, or just sitting together in silence. I love dancing with you, and how you're always able to find a song that fits exactly what we're going through at that moment. Most of all, I love how you hold me, and how you seem to know when words are not necessary, and when I just need to be held."

I couldn't stop smiling.

"Oh yeah, I forgot about your dimples, and your beautiful smile. You're also very HOT, with a capital H!" she said with confidence.

"Whew! Thank you, honey. By the way, this is one of those times when I'm taking control."

I lifted her in my arms and carried her up the stairs. As we entered the bedroom, I noticed there were candles on the chest of drawers and the nightstands. I sent up a silent thank you to Elaine, I knew this was her idea. I lit the candles, and slowly began undressing her. I kissed her after removing each piece of clothing. I began taking off my clothes. We both were very aroused, but I was taking this slow and easy. I picked her up and carried her to bed. I turned the music to a Lionel Richie song, called "Truly". As the song said, I was truly head over heels in love with her. I couldn't get enough of her, couldn't stop kissing her all over. She seemed to match my thoughts, and my moves. Forget slow and easy, I made love to her like there was no tomorrow. It seemed we couldn't get enough of each other. We both finally exploded! I kissed her long and hard, pulled her closer, and I held her.

Chapter 12

It was so good to have dinner with Joe and Elaine. Nicole and Elaine gushed like little girls, and Joe whispered in my ear, and said it's about time! Of course, wedding talk consumed most of the evening. Nicole and I had talked about it but had not yet set a date.

"By the way, Daniel, Elaine signed me up for a kickboxing class with her at the senior center. If I must suffer, so do you. Come along with us," Joe said, with amusement.

I chuckled under my breath because I was sure Nicole had no interest in kickboxing. I was shocked when I heard her say *"sign us up too, this will be fun."* I whipped my head around just in time to see her with a big smile on her face, or maybe it was a smirk. Time would tell.

Our first class was mostly the instructor showing us basic moves, and when and how to use them. I noticed Nicole was focused and following his every word. In the third class, we had to take a partner and show what we had learned so far. I asked Nicole to be my partner. I would go easy on her and make her look good.

Well, she kicked my butt! I was not expecting that! My ego was further bruised when Joe joked and said I better watch my back.

We had six more classes, and she continued to whip me. She got an award in the last class, so the four of us went to dinner to celebrate. She was glowing.

"You've done this before, haven't you, " I questioned.

"Just a few times," Nicole responded, with a timid smile.

"Define a few, for me," I said.

I could see Joe having a hard time holding his laughter in.

She gave me a sweet, innocent smile. Joe leaned in, and I heard him say, *"This should be good!"* Elaine shushed him, but she was also smiling and waiting for Nicole's response.

"I moved to Atlanta shortly after my divorce. The move and starting a new position was good for me, but once I got settled in, my emotions became front and center. I couldn't ignore them any longer. I knew I needed to do something, so I started seeing a counselor. I told her all I wanted to do was hit something, or somebody. She suggested that I redirect my anger and use it in a more positive way. Her brother taught kickboxing at the Y, and he agreed to give me private lessons. After a month, he said I should join his classes. I did that for four years, and in the last year, he let me assist him as an instructor."

My jaw dropped, and Joe burst out laughing.

I let go of my male ego and gave her a kiss on the cheek. I was so proud of her, but as Joe warned, I was going to watch my back from now on.

Chapter 13

Daniel's students were attending a career fair today. He thought it may involve some recruiting, and he wanted to be there for them. He was excited that two of them were getting a lot of notice. He asked me to meet him there so we could have lunch together. As I stood at the door looking for him, I heard someone call my name. I turned toward the voice. Oh gross, it was my ex. I almost didn't recognize him. He looked much older. I guess keeping up with a young child and a young wife was taking a toll on him. He tried to hug me, and I managed to step sideways just in time. I didn't want him to touch me.

"You look great, Nicole," Charles said, with confidence.

I started looking around. Where was Daniel?

Being Charles, he thought it was about him. "Don't worry, if you're looking for Lily, she's not here. She left me for a guy her age and took our son with her."

I really didn't need or want to hear this. At that moment I realized I was truly past all his crap. I had absolutely no thoughts or feelings as far as he was concerned. I wondered what I ever saw in him. That didn't stop him from talking.

"I've been meaning to call and check on you, see how you're doing," Charles said, with a bit of smugness.

At that moment, I felt Daniel's arm around my shoulder as he said, " No need, I've got that covered."

I noticed he had an alpha male stance, as if he were claiming his territory.

That still didn't stop Charles. He held out his hand, saying, "Charles Maxwell."

He said it with so much arrogance, almost as if he were royalty.

Daniel shook his hand, then leaned close to Charles and said something. I couldn't hear what he was saying, but I noticed Charles had a funny look on his face and his body stiffened.

"Come on honey, I want to introduce you to someone," Daniel said, as he took my hand and led me away.

As we walked away, I asked what that was all about.

"Nothing," Daniel said, "I just told him he would lose some body parts if I caught him hitting on you again."

"Do you know each other," I asked.

"We had an encounter once. I didn't make the connection with you and him, you don't have the same last name."

"No, I kept my maiden name when he and I married."

"Well, I don't trust him. When we get home, I'm updating your alarm system." Daniel firmly declared.

The look on his face told me this was not a time to question further.

We stayed close to home for several days. Daniel didn't mention Charles, and I thought it was best to table it for the moment as well.

At the end of the week, Daniel said we should go for a run and get some fresh air. I was more than ready.

We started along at a slow steady pace for the first mile. It felt good to be out in the park again. We picked up speed, and as we came around a bend, I saw a man jump out on the trail. On second look, I realized it was Charles, and he was holding a gun. He had a strange look on his face. Daniel motioned for me to keep running. I heard a yell, looked back, and saw that Daniel had kicked the gun out of Charles' hands. They were rolling on the ground punching each other. My hands were shaking as I held my cell phone, trying to get a signal. I walked a little further, hoping that would help. Suddenly, I heard a gunshot. I turned to run toward the sound when a lady jumped in front of me.

"Not so fast, missy," she said.

Oh my God!! It was Carolyn! We stared at each other. I knew I could easily outrun her. She must have read my mind. She reached into her jacket pocket and pulled out a gun. I knew I couldn't outrun a gun. Without a second thought, I flung my body towards her. It took her by surprise and the gun went flying across the trail. I punched her several times, and she fell to the ground. I kept punching her, then got up, and started kicking her. I was in a mad rage; my adrenaline was out of control. Suddenly, someone grabbed me from behind, picking me up. I kept kicking, then felt my body go limp.

$$\heartsuit$$

Chapter 14

I woke up in a bright, noisy room. I saw Joe standing at the foot of my bed, wearing scrubs. Daniel and Elaine were sitting on either side of my bed. The lights were hurting my eyes, and when I reached up to cover them, I noticed there was an IV in my left hand, and the right one was bandaged.

"Well, sleeping beauty is awake," I heard Joe say.

I was having a hard time concentrating. I couldn't figure out why I was here. I looked over at Daniel and saw bruises on his face, his lip was swollen. It all came back to me in a rush. I grabbed for the bedrail to escape, and realized I didn't have the strength. Daniel touched my shoulder and gently helped me lie back down. Tears started flowing from my eyes. I couldn't stop them. My heart was pounding, as if it was going to jump out of my chest. I heard Joe say they were going to admit me for observation, and shortly after, I felt the bed moving.

Elaine and Daniel remained by my side as I was taken to my room. They were making small talk and trying their best to keep me calm. Shortly after, a dinner tray arrived. I had no appetite and told Daniel to eat it. I was sure he had not left my side for hours. The nurse said I should at least drink, and that when I became more hydrated, they would remove the IV. I did as I was told, and it was a big relief to get rid of the IV. Shortly after, Elaine left, and promised to be back in the morning.

Daniel looked so tired, but he kept holding my hand and talking to me. I asked him to get in bed with me. He held me in his arms, and my tears started flowing again. Shortly after, Joe came in and gave me a shot. I felt like I was floating, and soon after, I was in a deep sleep.

I woke to bright light again, only this time it was the sun rising. Daniel was still holding me, and I could hear him snoring. He really needed the rest, so I tried to remain as still as possible. I felt calmer, and thankfully my heart had stopped pounding. I could feel myself drifting and didn't fight it. I fell asleep again.

I awoke to the smell of food. I can't believe I slept until noon. Daniel was sitting in the chair beside my bed. He had showered and changed clothes. He looked much better. The swelling on his face was getting better. Elaine was sitting on the other side of the bed reading. Joe stopped by to say hi. It was his day off, but he took another shift so he could keep an eye on me. My heart swelled to know I was surrounded by so much love.

The food was good, and I ate all of it. I was going to have more tests later, and if everything was ok, they would let me go home after dinner. Joe and Elaine went to lunch, and Daniel and I were finally alone. I was dying for some answers about yesterday's craziness.

"Daniel, what did you find out about Charles and Carolyn?" I asked.

"It's so crazy, I'm not sure where to begin. Feel free to interrupt at any time, it may help me piece everything together," Daniel responded and began the explanation.

"As you probably know, Charles and Lily are not together anymore."

"Yes, he said she left him for a younger man," I said.

"That's the story he tells. She left him because he was physically abusive. When she moved out of his house, he told her if he couldn't have her, no one else would. She tried getting help through the court system, but that made him angry, and more abusive. She became scared he would hurt their son, so she sent him to live with her parents. She hired an off-duty police officer to guard her," he continued.

"The officer had been following Charles for several weeks. Charles would drive up and down her street, but never stopped. Last week, he finally did. The officer sent her a code as Charles was pulling into the driveway. The idea was for her to come outside, so that she would be in full view. She said Charles looked strange, like maybe he was high. He told her she could go forward with the divorce, that he was going back to you,"

"What???" I yelled, not trying to control my shock. Daniel shook his head and continued with the story.

"He also told her he was taking up running as a way to bond better with you. She told the officer something didn't seem right. Luckily, he listened to her, and got two other officers to join him. One day they saw Charles and Carolyn having lunch. One of them overheard Charles saying it would be a win-win for them both. The officers didn't have a clue what that meant."

"Wait a minute," I said, "What was the connection with the two of them?"

"Remember me telling you I had an encounter with him? Well, years ago, Carolyn worked as his administrative assistant. One day she came home and told me Charles had made a pass at her. I asked her if she wanted me to go punch his lights out, and she said no, she loved the job. A few months later, she told me he had hit on her again and she had quit her job that day. I went down to have a man to man talk with him. Fortunately, someone came into the office as we were yelling at each other and about to exchange blows," Daniel explained.

"Oh, my goodness, I remember that! I helped him for two weeks until he could find another assistant. When I asked him where she went, he said her husband was jealous of him, and made her quit," I exclaimed with astonishment.

"Sounds like he was quite a creative liar," Daniel added.

"My goodness, Daniel, this sounds like something out of late-night TV." I said just before Daniel continued the story.

"Yes, it does! They had followed Charles to the park three days in a row. He just sat in the car. Evidently, he was waiting for us to show up. On the day we finally showed up, they saw us get out of the car, but of course they didn't know who we were. Charles left and drove to another park entrance."

"What was the gun shot I heard?" I asked, trying to get all the details.

Daniel continued the story, "That was the officer. They split up and started walking around the area. Charles had slipped away from them, and that was when he ran into us. While he and I were beating the crap out of each other, one of the officers showed up and shot in the air to stop us."

"So, what was Carolyn's part," I asked, with disbelief in their stupidity.

Daniel had more details to give me first, "Carolyn had parked at another entrance, close to the bathroom. She stayed in there a while, then Charles texted her to come out, and activate their plan."

"What idiots! Where are they now?" I frantically asked.

"Charles is in jail. Lily added to his woes, and decided to press charges for the times he abused her. She turned out to be quite clever, and had cameras installed inside the house. He was caught red handed. He had a lot of bruises and a broken nose from our fight, but otherwise he was ok. He will be in there for a while. Carolyn turned against him and told everything,"

"Daniel, I'm still having a hard time understanding all of this." I stated because he had not revealed Charles and Carolyn's plan.

"From what Carolyn told the police, the plan, according to Charles, was to scare you and me from each other and back to them. Charles called that a win-win. Carolyn figured out the real plan was for Charles to kill me, assuming that would make you run back to him," Daniel summed it up for me.

"Oh, my goodness!" I said, at a loss for words.

"She is currently in a room in another part of the hospital. She didn't fare as well as he did. She has a broken jaw, broken ribs, and a ruptured spleen. Once the officer separated Charles and me, I took off running in the direction you had gone. I saw you beating up on Carolyn. Before I could get to you, the second officer came from a different direction and pulled you off her. Remind me not to ever make you mad," Daniel said with a slight grin on his face.

♡
Chapter 15

My test results were negative, and I was able to go home that evening. The doctors were mainly concerned that I could have a mild concussion. Thankfully, that was not the case. They also removed the bandage from my hand. My knuckles were badly bruised, but no fracture.

It was so good to be home, and to sleep in my own bed. I went to bed early, leaving Daniel in the living room watching a football game. I woke up briefly when he came to bed, then went back into a sound sleep.

Sometime during the night, I heard a noise. I looked up and saw Carolyn coming toward me. Oh gosh, I thought Daniel told me she was in the hospital. I took off running, but she quickly caught up. I started screaming at her and flinging my arms in the air. My heart was racing. She grabbed me from behind, as if she were giving me a bear hug. I was kicking and screaming as hard as I could. Then

I heard Daniel calling my name, and realized I was having a bad dream. He pulled me closer and held me in his arms. He was talking, but I couldn't make out the words. I started crying and couldn't stop. He turned me towards him so I could see his face. I continued crying. He kept holding me, until I finally settled down and went back to sleep.

I made breakfast the next morning. We didn't talk much while eating, but I did notice Daniel looked very concerned.

I began to cry, as I said, "Daniel, I can't do this."

"Do what, honey?"

"I need to step back and work on what's going on inside of me," I blubbered, as the tears flowed freely.

He had a bewildered look, which I totally understood, because I didn't know what I was saying either.

"Whatever is going on, we can work it out together," Daniel pleaded.

I slid the ring off my finger and placed it in his hand.

"Are you breaking our engagement?" he asked, with a shocked look.

"I'm just taking a break to heal. When I accepted your proposal, and the ring, I made a promise to you. At this moment, I'm not doing a good job of fulfilling that promise," I said in shame.

We looked at each other, and I started crying again. Daniel turned his head, but not before I noticed the emotion in his eyes.

"I don't want to leave you alone like this," he said.

"I'll call Elaine if I need anything." I wanted to reach for his hand, to help heal the pain I knew I was causing.

At that moment, I didn't have the energy to help either of us heal.

He was still holding the ring in his hand. He looked at it, then looked at me, and quietly put the ring in his pocket.

My tears were flowing like a river, and he asked if he could give me a hug. I couldn't get the words out, so I just nodded. He pulled me into his arms and held me. We stood that way for a while. When he pulled back, I noticed he had tears in his eyes. That made me cry even more.

"Nicole, I made a promise to you, too. I will end the day with a text. When you are ready to talk, I'll always be here for you. I gave you my heart, and I want you to keep it. Without you in my life, it's no good to me."

He kissed my forehead, and quietly slipped out the door.

I wanted to curl up into a little ball and cry myself to sleep.

I knew I needed help and remembered Joe giving me a business card for a counselor. I emptied the contents of my purse on the table, and searched until I found the card. Her personal cell number was written in Joe's neat handwriting. I thought I would take a chance. She answered on the second ring, almost as if she were expecting my call. I asked if I could make an appointment with her. To my surprise, she answered, "Your timing is perfect; I had a lunch class for today, which just got canceled. Why don't I drop by to see you, and bring lunch? I heard you love turkey burgers, and I know a wonderful place to get them."

I gave a sigh of relief and thanked her profusely.

Dr. Matthews came by several hours later, with a bag filled with delicious smelling goodies.

As I led her to the kitchen, she said "I have two rules – first, please call me Holly, instead of Dr. Matthews. Second rule is, we eat first, and talk business after."

I liked her style, which put me at ease right away.

The food was delicious! I can't wait to tell Daniel about the place. It took a while, but he finally took a liking to turkey instead of beef.

Holly listened without interrupting, as I told her about the events of the last week or so. I told her how emotional I was, and how I couldn't stop crying. I told her about the nightmares, the racing heart, and finally, about Daniel.

"From everything you've told me, it sounds like a classic case of post-traumatic stress," Holly said.

"I always thought that was for soldiers, or people involved in a war," I said.

Holly nodded in agreeance, and said, "You're correct, there is a lot of it in that sector, but anyone can have symptoms of it after a trauma such as what you've experienced,"

"It makes perfect sense, now that you put it that way," I finally began to feel the load on my shoulders lighten a little.

"How is your sleeping?" Holly asked.

"Not good. I'll sleep for a few hours but wake up feeling like I've just run a marathon," I answered.

Holly reached into her pocket and pulled out a small box, "Joe told me you don't like taking meds, so I picked this up at the drugstore on my way here. It's a natural essential oil, which will calm you and help you sleep. You will not feel drugged even if you wake up in the middle of the night. I use it myself."

"I feel better already. I don't know why I didn't think of what my symptoms could mean. Thank you so much," I responded.

"Don't kick yourself too much, Nicole. It's hard sometimes to think straight when you're in the middle of something like this. Let's call it a day and meet again tomorrow. I'll bring pizza for lunch," Holly concluded before leaving.

When she left, I felt like the weight of the world was beginning to drop from my shoulders. I did some house cleaning, and even had enough energy to wash the car.

That night, I took a long bubble bath. As I was drying off, I heard my phone buzz. It was a text from Daniel with an emoji of a heart. I usually text him in the mornings, but I responded right away with two hearts. I felt lighter, and realized I had not cried, or felt like crying since that morning. I rubbed the essential oil on my wrists and had a great night's sleep.

Holly dropped by the next day with two boxes of pizza. I hadn't eaten pizza in a long time, this was a special treat.

She asked if I'd ever heard of a flight or fight response.

I nodded that I had heard of it.

She went into more detail, explaining how I experienced that when I was beating the crap out of Carolyn. The only thing was, I never came out of that mode, which explains the feelings and lack of control I've been having. She gave me an exercise routine which would help. I was feeling much stronger.

She said we only needed one more session, and we would talk about Daniel. I offered to bring her lunch this time. I really needed to get out of this house.

That night, Daniel sent a text saying he loved me. I responded saying I loved him more.

Another good night's sleep, and I was ready for my session with Holly. I picked up lunch and headed to her office. After stuffing ourselves, she said it was time to talk about Daniel. She asked me to start from the beginning. That was easy to do. I told her everything – my feelings, how wonderful and thoughtful he was, how he listened to me, how creative his surprises were. She asked about his proposal. I was getting emotional telling her about our magical week in Jamaica, how he made my birthday so special, and ended the day with his proposal. I ended by telling her about giving the ring back.

"It sounds like he's a keeper. It also sounds like you love each other very much. Are you having any more of the symptoms we've talked about the last few days?" asked Holly.

When I told her no, she was pleased. She said we didn't need the formal sessions anymore, and I could call anytime I needed her. I thanked her again and gave her a big hug. As I walked out of her office, I knew exactly what I needed to do.

Chapter 16

The last few days had been the hardest I've ever experienced. I missed Nicole so much. When she gave me the ring back, I felt so lost. I drove home and sat in the car wondering what had gone wrong. I stayed to myself at first, and finally called Joe last night to talk. He invited me to lunch today at some new place he heard about. He said it's called The Burger Barn. He chuckled and said not to worry, I could get a turkey burger there. He found every chance he could to joke about my not eating beef anymore.

I awoke early, washed clothes, and cleaned the kitchen and bathrooms. It felt good to be doing some-thing constructive. I thought keeping busy would keep my mind off Nicole. That didn't work, she was always foremost in my thoughts. I turned the music on, but every song reminded me of her. Boy, I had it bad! It hurt me to see her crying and so emotional. It hurt even more that I didn't seem to be much help. I thought maybe writing my thoughts would help, so I began what ended up being a love note to her. I must admit, I did feel better when I was finished. Maybe one day, I'll give her the note, but for now, I'll keep it to myself. She really doesn't need anything else to trigger her emotions. I thought of going to one of our support group meetings, they were helpful in the past. In the end, I decided not to do it.

I saw Joe's car right away when I pulled into the parking lot of The Burger Barn. I had never heard of it before, and hoped the food was good. Suddenly, I realized how hungry I was. I walked around looking for Joe, and finally saw him waving at me from a booth in the back of the room. Once I got closer, I realized he was not alone. Our pastor, Bill Richards, was sitting across from him. Bill was also one of the founders of our support group. I was glad to see them both, they must have read my mind. We talked about football until our food arrived. At that point, all talk stopped as we stuffed ourselves. The food was very good. I couldn't wait to tell Nicole about it.

Bill started the ball rolling by asking how I was doing. It was my time to vent so I did just that.

"To be honest with you, Bill, I don't know. So much is going around in my mind, and I can't make it slow down enough to get a grip on things. I've managed to push Charles and Carolyn to the back of my mind, I know the court will handle them. Nicole is different, she's always my first thought, and I'm at a loss as to how to help her.

I'm having a hard time understanding why she's pushing me away. I want to be her shoulder to lean on, her rock, and she doesn't seem to want or need that,"

Bill raised his index finger and said, "Hold on to that thought, and we'll come back to it. For now, I want you to tell me five things you love the most about Nicole."

I sat up and professed, "That's easy – I love her mind, her intelligence. I love that she constantly challenges herself, and me, to be the best we can be. I love how independent she is, how she knows when to solve things on her own, and when she needs to reach out for me to hold her hand. I love the sophisticated woman she is, as well as the giddy five-year-old girl in her. Most of all, I love how she puts me first, how she makes sure I'm eating properly, and getting my rest."

"I think you're on to something. Just one more question, how did Nicole get into kickboxing," Bill asked.

I wasn't sure what that had to do with anything, so I thought about it for a bit. Then it hit me like a smack on the head. I then said, "She started it when she felt like she couldn't handle her emotions after her divorce."

"You nailed it! Think about this – perhaps Nicole is so overwhelmed with her emotions, she doesn't know where to begin. You said she puts you first. Is it possible she's doing that now, even as she's hurting?" asked Bill.

"How?" I responded in a state of confusion.

Bill could see the confusion on my face and answered, "You both just had a very traumatic experience. Naturally, you're concerned about Nicole, while at the same time, you're pushing your feelings to the side. Not a bad thing at all, but you're so worried about Nicole that you're not facing your own issues. Does that make sense?"

"You're right, Bill, and yes, it makes perfect sense," I stated feeling hopeful.

Bill continued with a profound rhetorical question, "Could it be Nicole is working on herself as we speak, and also preparing for when it will fully hit you, and she will need to be your strength, your rock, as you say?"

"Oh my God, you're exactly right! Why didn't I think of that myself?" I exclaimed in astonishment.

"Sometimes it's hard to think logically when you're in the middle of a difficult situation. I have one more thing to show you," Bill stated.

He started a video on his cell phone. There was no sound, and I had a hard time following at first. Then I realized it was a video from the surveillance camera at the park. It was Nicole fighting Carolyn. She was putting so much into her fight, as if her life, and possibly mine, depended on it. She was fighting like a Mama Bear protecting her cub. Even after the officer pulled her away, she continued the fight.

"Wow!" I couldn't hide my shock.

"Now do you see why she felt she needed to take a step back? She's not leaving you; she's working on preserving your future together. It's such a natural thing for her that she may or may not see it that way yet. The love you have for each other is obvious to everyone around you. You both glow like neon lights," Bill said, with a chuckle.

"Thank you so much for opening my eyes. I'm sorry to cut this lunch short, but I know what I need to do," I said as I had devised a plan.

"Go after the woman you love. Once you two get it together, I would be honored to perform your wedding ceremony," Bill declared.

As I was leaving, I heard Joe say he would give me away. That made me smile. I truly have the best friends.

Chapter 17

I jumped in the car and whipped out of the parking lot. I wanted to make a quick stop home, then go after my lady. As I was coming down the stairs, I heard the doorbell ring. Dang, I didn't have time for that right now. I ran to the door and yanked it open. There stood Nicole!

I held out my hand, she took it, and we hugged each other. She was the first to let go.

She looked at me with that beautiful smile, and said "Daniel, I was wrong, and I'm sorry."

"Come have a seat, let me have your jacket," I said.

"You have your jacket on too, were you going out?" she asked.

"Actually, I was on my way to your house Nicole. I just had lunch with Joe and Pastor Bill, and they helped me see some things clearer. I decided I didn't want to go another day with the distance between us. I had to run home first, and I'm glad I did, otherwise we would've missed each other. Please tell me why you think you were wrong,"

"Early in our relationship, you asked that we talk if things weren't working between us. I didn't give you that chance. I am so sorry I pushed you away," she responded.

I held her hand. "Fill me in on what's been going on with you the last few days."

She told me about the sessions with Dr. Holly, about the post-traumatic stress, and Holly's theory of why it was taking a while to get through it.

"It hurt me badly to see you so emotional and crying without control. I felt helpless, because I feel it's my responsibility to be your shoulder to lean on, and there was nothing I could do. I'm glad you got help when you realized you couldn't get a grip on your emotions. Bill helped me see that even though you were drowning in pain, you were also thinking about me. He believes you sensed I was ignoring my pain, and that you knew it would surface one day. I now know you weren't pushing me away; you were trying to get yourself together so you could be there for me. There is no reason to apologize, you were having feelings and emotions that are completely foreign to you. When I look back, I realize how hard you fought those emotions, and how hard it was for you to give the ring back. I know I've told you this many times, but I've got to say again how much I admire your strength. You are the person I want and need by my side, in good times, or bad." I hugged her as tightly as I could. I needed to feel our hearts beating together, and in sync. I wanted to offer her some reassurance.

"It's good that we both got help. There is one more thing we need to do, and nobody else can help us with this part. We need to go back to the park and face our fears."

"I'm scared," she said.

"I know you are. I am too. We're a team, you've got my back, and I've got yours. I know there are other parks in town, but this is the one that means the most to us. You've told me many times that it's your happy place. I want it to be that way again, for us both," I continued to reassure Nicole.

"Ok, I guess we should get it over with," she exhaled.

"Just one more thing before we go," I said while reaching into my pocket to pull out her ring. I slid it on her finger while holding her hand securely in mine. I needed her to know she was always safe in my hands. She started crying, and I kissed her forehead.

"Don't worry, these are good tears this time," Nicole said with a small chuckle.

I breathed a sigh of relief, as I hugged her.

"Nicole, every day I fall more in love with you. You have captured my heart, body, and soul, and I give them all up willingly. I need you in my life, by my side. Will you marry me?" I asked.

She was nodding her head as the tears rolled down her face. I tried my best to wipe her tears away.

"Honey, I can't hear you when you nod. I need to hear the words out loud."

"Yes, yes I will marry you! I will be by your side, holding your hand as we enjoy our future together. Daniel, I love you so much!"

"One more thing, I would like to get married as soon as possible. I know you don't want a formal wedding. What about if we go downtown on Monday and apply for a marriage license? Pastor Bill told me today he would be happy to officiate. We can't leave out Joe and Elaine. They would like to give us a reception. It can be a small, intimate one, if that makes you happiest. What do you think," I asked.

"Let's do it! How about three weeks from now? That way Elaine doesn't have too much time to go overboard," she said this with a chuckle.

"It's a date! Will you take my name, will you be Mrs. Washington?"

"It would be an honor."

"Thank you. By the way, I sent you some flowers, which will be delivered this evening. I figured if I came by and you wouldn't let me in, the flowers would be my way of ending the day on a good note."

"That's why I love you so much," she said with a smile.

"Let's go to the park now. Then we can get on with the rest of our lives," I took her hand and led her out the door.

$\heartsuit$

Chapter 18

We drove to the park and sat in the car for a few minutes. So far, so good. We opened our doors at the same time and started walking toward the trails. We looked at each other and smiled, as we held hands and walked in silence. Nicole tightened her grip on my hand, but no tears. We approached a bench and decided to sit down.

"Honey, your mind seems to be twirling. What are you thinking about," I asked, with a look of concern.

"Just random thoughts going through my mind, mostly good, though. Daniel, I'm thankful for you suggesting we come back here. I don't think I ever would have come back. It hasn't been as bad as I thought it would be."

"Well, let's keep going. We can stop whenever you want to. If we need to, we can come back tomorrow and continue this journey."

"I'm ok, let's go," Nicole responded showing her strength.

We both did fine until we got to the part of the trail where we had encountered Charles. I heard Nicole gasp for breath. I noticed tears were flowing down her face. My heart was racing, and I felt close to tears myself. We stood still for a few moments, then, to my surprise, she reached out, pulled me towards her, and she held me. Time seemed to stand still. The birds were chirping, and from a distance, I could hear people walking on the surrounding trails. She continued to hold me. My heart rate began to slow down. I felt like I could breathe normally again. And she held me.

After a while, we pulled apart, smiled at each other, and continued walking. There was no need for words. We walked a little further. I knew exactly what Nicole had in mind. It was her moment, and I was not going to interrupt. She picked up a huge rock, and a big stick from under the trees on the side of the trail. She put the rock down and stood in front of it. I could hear her mumbling to herself. I watched in silence. After a while, she looked up, almost as if she had just remembered that I was there. As she plunged the stick in the ground, I heard her say, "I came, I saw, I conquered!" We were at the spot where she had run into Carolyn. This was her way of claiming her life back. I was so proud of her. She wiped away her tears and gave me the biggest smile. I walked forward, pulled her toward me, and I held her.

As we began our walk back down the trail, Nicole said, "I have an idea. We can talk about it when we get to the car."

AND I HELD HER

Once we were settled in the car, I asked what her idea was.

"Have you ever noticed the benches in the park have little plaques with names on them," she asked.

"I've noticed it, but never really gave it much thought." I answered.

"Well, people donate to the parks, and their donations go towards many things. The benches are one of them. You and I are usually running, but did you notice how many people were sitting on the benches when we were coming down the trail?" she asked.

"Yes, I did," still waiting to hear her idea.

"Well, I want us to make a donation for a bench with our name on it."

"I like that idea. How should we put our name on the plaque?" I asked.

"#Team Washington, of course," she exclaimed.

We gave each other a fist bump. What a team we were! I started the car, and we headed home.

As we pulled into Nicole's driveway, the truck from the florist was right behind us. Talk about timing. I looked over at Nicole, and she had that giddy five- year-old look on her face. I loved that look.

We cooked dinner together, and I cleaned up afterwards. She sat at the table and kept looking at me and smiling. I know I had a big grin on my face too.

We had a few phone calls to make, and then we would be able to settle down and enjoy each other. Our first call was to Bill, to let him know we had set a date. He put his wife, Cheryl, on the phone, and she and Nicole giggled like little girls. They were so excited for us. He said they would be calling Joe and Elaine in the morning to get the ball rolling.

Our next call was to Joe and Elaine. After more girlish giggling, Nicole and Elaine agreed to meet for lunch the next day. Nicole had very specific thoughts of how she wanted our big day to be.

Now, it was our time to sit and relax. Music was playing softly in the background. Nicole snuggled close to me and rested her head on my shoulder. What a day this has been. It was very emotional but ended well. Pretty soon, we both were nodding, and having a hard time keeping our eyes open. I didn't realize how tired I was, and Nicole was looking the same way.

We showered together and went to bed. I pulled her toward me, kissed her, and held her in my arms all night. There was no other place I wanted to be.

Chapter 19

$\mathcal{I}$t had been a busy three weeks, and finally, it was our wedding day. The sun was shining brightly, and the weather forecast was in our favor as well. It was going to be a beautiful day. Daniel and I agreed not to see each other until the ceremony. I was surprised at how much I missed him. He sent his usual nightly text last night, but I gave in first and called him. We talked for two hours. He gave in this morning and called me first. We were both counting down the hours.

We decided to have a quiet dinner instead of a big reception. The last few months were difficult, but as hard as it had been, we learned so much about ourselves and about each other. We really were a team, with a wonderful support group. Pastor Bill offered to have the dinner at their home. Of course, Joe and Elaine, our biggest fans, would be there, as would Dr. Holly and her friend Andrew. We may have a reception in the future, but for now, this would be fine.

Daniel found the perfect mountain retreat for our honeymoon. I wasn't thinking of a honeymoon when I suggested we get married in three weeks. I'm always amazed at how he pulls things together so fast. We're looking forward to getting out of town for a few days. We decided we would go back to Jamaica in a few months for the holidays.

I heard the doorbell ring, and when I answered, there stood Elaine, Cheryl, and Holly. They said they came to kidnap me and take me to breakfast. We had a fun time together. I was surprised how hungry I was. Elaine said the guys were together, probably roasting Daniel.

"Daniel was Joe's best man at our wedding. He gave Joe a hard time, so I'm sure it will be payback time," Elaine said.

"I love their relationship. They're closer than some brothers I know," I said, with a smile.

Elaine confirmed, "True, Joe said when they were in college, Daniel was the serious and focused one. The other guys in their fraternity used to call him the poet, but the girls called him the romantic. The guys would tease him and ask how an engineer could be considered romantic. According to them, engineers were boring and had no imagination."

"I think Daniel's romantic nature is one of my favorite things about him. It was hard at first, because I've never been an emotional person, and I usually hung around people a lot like me. He has really taught me how to feel and express my emotions. I think sometimes, like today, I go overboard with the feelings because they're so unnatural for me," I confessed.

· Holly and Cheryl piped in and said not to worry, I was doing a great job.

When I turned toward Holly, I noticed a ring on her left hand.

"By the way Holly, what is that rock on your finger," I asked, relieved to get the focus from me.

She blushed and said, "I didn't want to say anything because it's your day. Andrew proposed to me last night."

"That is awesome! Congratulations, Holly. Ladies, let's have a group hug."

Shortly after, they took me home. They would be back in a few hours to pick me up and take me to Cheryl and Bill's home. I couldn't stop smiling as I got dressed for our big day. I couldn't wait to see Daniel.

Daniel's car was the first thing I noticed when we pulled in the driveway. I felt my heart skip a beat.

We walked to Bill's home office, only to find the door closed. Cheryl said she was sure the guys were in there, so I knocked. The door opened and Daniel was standing there, a huge grin on his face. He took my hand and escorted me into the room. The other ladies thought that was so sweet, but I was sure they had planned it.

Bill performed the ceremony, and we said our vows. Daniel and I kept looking at each other. Thankfully, there wouldn't be a test later because I didn't remember much. At last, Bill pronounced us husband and wife. Daniel and I had goofy grins on our faces. He whispered I love you in my ear and kissed me. I felt like I was in heaven. We hugged each other, until we heard Joe clearing his throat.

Joe chuckled and said, "Hey buddy, I know you're

anxious to have your first dance with your wife, but, well you know what they say about payback. You're going to have to listen to me talk a bit."

Elaine smacked his hand, and that got a laugh out of all of us.

We went to another room, which was beautifully decorated. Elaine and her crew did an awesome job. There were two chairs in the center of the room for us. Daniel pulled them closer together, and we held hands.

Joe came forward, shook Daniel's hand, and gave me a kiss on the cheek. He then began his testimonial to us.

"Daniel and Nicole, we are so happy for you. I can honestly say I've never seen a couple complement each other the way you do. Nicole, thank you for coming into my brother's life and turning it upside down, in the best way. We knew he was smitten when a bunch of us guys went to lunch at a steak house, and he ordered a salad. We got a good laugh at his expense, but it didn't seem to faze him. Then, the care and attention he put into building the house for your holiday surprise last year was the biggest sign. Who knew engineers had so much imagination?" He paused briefly to let out a chuckle and continued in a more serious tone.

"My favorite thing about you is the way you love and care about each other. You realize a good relationship is not about perfection, it's about accepting each other's faults, and not letting them get in your way. You are both very strong-willed, analytical people. Yet, you are in tune with each other. You seem to know who needs the other's shoulder, and you lend it, no discussion. It's an automatic thing for you two. Daniel, I've seen the alpha male in you, and Nicole, I've seen the Mama Bear in you. You are very protective of each other, yet so gentle with each other," Joe briefly paused again but it seemed like he was holding back tears this time.

"Daniel, I know you chose a romantic love song for your first dance. You can save that for later when you're alone. I flipped the script a bit and chose a song that I believe is the epitome of the love you share. The song is called "It Takes Two," by Marvin Gaye and Kim Weston. As the song says, it takes two to make a dream come true. It's a song about two people who complement and complete each other. That is you! You truly have each other's back. What a formidable team you are! Now, you may have your first dance together as husband and wife."

As we started our dance, Daniel wiped a tear that rolled down my cheek. He whispered the words to the song in my ear as we danced. I felt like we were alone in our own little world.

The others soon joined us, and we danced to several more songs.

The caterers were busy in the kitchen and said dinner would be ready in 30 minutes.

Daniel asked for everyone's attention, as he began to speak.

"My wife and I would like to thank all of you for this wonderful day. You helped make it so special. Now, we have a wedding gift for you. There are two parts to it, and Nicole will start."

"Daniel and I are so happy to spend today with you. I

always say it takes a village to get anything done properly. Thank you for being our village, and for your love and support, especially the last few months. Thank you for being a part of #Team Washington. Daniel just gave you an envelope. Please open them and look at the pictures inside. You will see four benches in the park. The center one says #Team Washington, and the surrounding three have a plague with each of your names. This is our village and will remain a part of the park. Now, I'll let my husband give you the second part," I gushed, realizing how much I loved calling him my husband.

There was a round of applause, and hugs shared. Daniel then began speaking again as we had one more part of the gift for our village.

"I'm not sure how Nicole got all this accomplished, but she did it in three weeks. This was a labor of love for her, and she even had me out there last night planting flowers. Now, for my part. Nicole will give you an envelope. Inside, you will find two things. The first is for a two week stay at our home in Jamaica, and the second is a voucher for a plane ticket to get there. They're good for any time you want to go. Again, thank you all for your love and support."

There were hugs all around, and then we went into the dining room for dinner. Shortly after dinner, Daniel and I were ready to go home. This day had been filled with so much love. Now we were ready to relax and spend time alone.

Chapter 20

On our way home, I couldn't resist teasing Daniel. "So, I heard you were called the romantic in college," I said, with a smirk.

He smiled and showed those dimples that I love. Daniel began to tell me the story.

"I guess I'll never live that down. In my first year of college, I wrote a love poem to the girl I was dating. She showed it to her friends. They showed it to their boyfriends, and asked why they couldn't be romantic like that. After that year, I really knuckled down and concentrated hard on my classes, but I think writing that poem will follow me forever. The thing is, the poem wasn't my own creation. I've always loved music, so I just took lines from different songs, and made it into a poem. Guys are always complaining about how hard it is to understand you women. If we take the time to learn your personalities, it's quite easy to charm you."

"Oh really! You're revealing your secrets now that I have your name, "I giggled, with amusement.

"And my heart honey, you got my heart, too!" Daniel affirmed.

"Uh Huh! Well, it looks like you have been saved for the moment, since we're home," I giggled more.

He picked me up and carried me into the house. Even though we've spent so much time here, this moment felt so magical.

As music played in the background, we talked about our favorite parts of the day.

"Elaine said you and the guys spent the morning together. What did you do," I inquired.

Daniel told me all about it, "Joe came by and said we were to meet Bill and Andrew for breakfast. Once we got there, four of our frat brothers were there. They spent the next hour roasting me. I know I deserved most of it, so I took it in stride. The other guys only seem to remember the jokes I played on them, never the things they did to me,"

"Really, what kind of jokes did you play?" I asked.

"Joe is always joking about how I've been acting like a lovesick teenager since I met you. You should've seen him when he first met Elaine. In the beginning of their relationship, he dropped out of sight for a while. I waited until a night I knew he was working in the ER and got one of my friends from the police department to go by the hospital and do a welfare check on him," Daniel continued.

"You really were bad!" I exclaimed.

"Yeah, I was, but I made up for it. I let him spend a week in the house in Jamaica. In fact, he proposed to Elaine there. They've been back several times since then." Daniel answered.

"Wow, Elaine didn't tell me about that,"

"I know, I asked her not to. I was afraid you two would start talking, and Elaine would give up too much information. I know how your investigative side is, and I didn't want my birthday surprise for you to be ruined."

"You're a really nice guy, and I'm not saying that because I happen to be married to you. You are so kind and so thoughtful. Your jokes and your surprises are very elaborate. I don't know how you manage to get other people involved and no one ever spills the beans," I said, with awe.

"I'll keep some secrets to myself. What did you think of Joe's speech?" Daniel asked.

"I loved it! It was so touching, and I learned something about us,"

Daniel looked confused and asked, "Really, what did you learn?"

I immediately offered my perspective, "It was an eye opener when Joe talked about how protective we are of each other, and how we seem to know when the other needs a shoulder to lean on."

Daniel finally expressed his feeling to me concerning the past event, "It seems he, Bill, and Holly worked together on the speech. I remember Bill telling me you probably sensed I was hiding my feelings about the incident with Charles and Carolyn, and that you were working on yourself because you knew it would hit me, and I would

[89]

need your shoulder. You demonstrated that the day we went back to the park after the incident. I wasn't expecting the feelings I had when we got to the spot where we had run into Charles. I saw you crying, and was trying to get to you, but I felt paralyzed. So much was going through my mind, my heart was racing, and I just couldn't move. When you reached out and took me in your arms, I felt myself calming down, and it seemed like all was finally right in our world."

"I never really gave it much thought. I knew you were hurting, and I wanted to be there for you, just as you've always done for me. It just seems like a natural thing to do. I also like the song Joe chose for us, and the reasons he said he chose it. What about the song he said you had chosen?"

"I'll save that for tomorrow, when we're in the mountains. For tonight, I want it to be about you and me. I want any words you remember to be from my heart, and not from a song. Are you ready for bed?" Daniel asked as he reached out his hand.

We held hands as we walked down the hall to the bedroom. I had left the door closed and had placed a sign on it which said #Team Washington. We smiled at each other as we went in.

The room was decorated with heart shaped balloons. Candles were all over, just waiting to be lit.

"So, Mr. Washington, would you like to take a shower, or a bubble bath, "I asked, as I flirted with him.

"Well, Mrs. Washington, it's your moment, I'll do whatever you say," Daniel responded following my lead.

"Hmm, I choose a shower, that way I can get a good look at your sexy body," I said.

"Nicole, are you flirting with me?" he asked, trying to look shocked.

"Yes I am. Lean forward so I can whisper in your ear and tell you exactly what I'm going to do to you." I whispered in his ear.

"Whew, honey, let's um, let's get the shower over with!" Daniel said in full excitement.

After our shower, I turned off the lights, and lit the candles. Smooth jazz was playing in the background. Daniel walked out of the bathroom with his towel wrapped around his waist. He smiled as he walked toward me. I yanked his towel off and pushed him on the bed. I took off my robe and laid beside him. I pulled his body close to mine and started kissing him. My hands wandered all over his body. I kissed his ears, his face, and slowly made my way down his entire body. When I felt he couldn't take any more teasing, I straddled him. Our bodies moved together in a slow, synchronous motion. I kissed him as I slowly made love to him. Then, he took over, flipped me on my back, and things sped up. The world stood still as we made love to each other.

"Damn honey," he said, as he pulled me into his arms. He kissed me and fell asleep. I followed soon after.

A few hours later, I woke up and saw Daniel sitting on the edge of the bed.

"Are you ok?" I asked.

"I'm hungry, do you want some breakfast?" He asked.

I offered him a different option, "It's only 3 a.m. How about I make you a grilled cheese sandwich, with a glass of milk to go with it?"

"Sounds good," he agreed.

It only took a few minutes to fix the sandwich, and he seemed happy.

"You know, honey, I know I've spent a lot of nights here, but last night felt different."

"I was thinking the same thing earlier. Even though we spent a lot of nights together, we never really lived together. Now that it's permanent, it's a good feeling, but like you said, it feels different. When we come back from the mountains, why don't we move more of your things in? The loft would be a perfect man cave for you. I only have a few things up there, which I can move to one of the bedrooms. I want you to feel like this is your home too."

"That sounds great, but maybe I should hold on to my house, in case you get mad one day and kick me out," he joked.

"I'm much more mature than that. I would never kick you out, I'll just make you sleep in the shed in the back yard," I responded, with a giggle.

The look on his face was priceless.

"I'm just kidding! Come on, let's go back to bed. We have a long drive later this morning, and I want you to get more rest."

Chapter 21

The smell of breakfast woke me from a deep sleep. Nicole was right, I needed the extra rest. A few hours later, we were on the road. She packed a picnic lunch, even though it was only a two-hour drive. I know how she likes to stop and take pictures everywhere we go, so I didn't say anything. It was a beautiful ride up the mountain, and the leaf colors were so brilliant this year. We stopped, ate lunch, and just enjoyed the views. I couldn't wait for her to see the cabin we would be staying in. I was at my wits end trying to plan the perfect honeymoon, and I only had a few weeks to get everything together. Thank goodness for good friends. Bill had a friend who agreed to let us stay in his cabin. We all worked together to make it the perfect honeymoon getaway. I wasn't planning on leaving the cabin until we headed back home.

I drove up a hill, and around the bend, and there stood the cabin. It looked nice from the outside. The area had a private feel to it since the nearest neighbor was half a mile away. I could tell Nicole loved it. She was having a hard time controlling her inner giddy five-year-old.

Before she had a chance to get out of the car, I ran around and opened the door for her. She kissed me on the cheek.

"Let's leave the bags in the car while we look around," I said.

The house was beautiful inside. There was a box on the kitchen counter with our names on it.

"Daniel, what do you think that is?" Nicole asked.

"Open it, so we can see," I said.

"Oh, my goodness! This is beautiful," she gushed, like a little girl.

Inside the box was a wedding cake. It was a replica of the house I built for our holiday gift exchange last year. There was a red heart on the front door. Over the heart, the words, *"The best is yet to come"* were written in black icing.

The caterer had left plenty of food in the refrigerator. All we had to do was heat it in the microwave. I could tell Nicole was having a hard time containing her excitement.

We sat down to eat a delicious meal of grilled salmon, coconut rice, green beans sauteed in garlic, and a salad. We let that settle, then ate a piece of the wedding cake. It was good. A few more days of eating like this, and I would need to run twice a day.

"Are you ready to see the rest of house," I asked.

She nodded, and I held her hand as we walked down the hallway. The bedroom door was closed. On the door was a big red heart with our names on it. Inside, rose petals in the shape of a heart covered the bed. There was a jacuzzi tub in the bathroom. It was surrounded by candles. I pushed a button on the wall, and the sound of smooth jazz began. I turned to Nicole, gave a slight bow, and asked her to dance with me. She wrapped her arms around my waist, and we held each other tightly.

We danced a few minutes, then sat down to relax. Tears were forming in her eyes. I kissed the side of her face, as if I were kissing the tears away. I gently said to her, "Honey, I know those are happy tears. I want you to know I'm always here to wipe your tears away, happy, or not. When you have a bad day, I promise I will try to help you have a better night. I'm right by your side, today, and always. You make me happier than I've ever been. I'm a very lucky man."

I took her right hand and matched it with my left one. I intertwined our fingers. At that moment, we were one. I leaned forward to kiss her.

"You really are a romantic man. I feel like I'm the lucky one. By the way, are you still using your charm on me?" she asked with a smile.

"Nah, I've already completely charmed you. I'm just maintaining it now," I said, with a grin.

"Will you kiss me again?"

"My pleasure. Nicole, I feel like we've been on a natural high for a long time. I don't want to come down. I know there will come a time when we disagree, maybe even argue. We're both very hardheaded and stubborn. When that time comes, please don't shut me out. I know that when you're upset, you go inward and analyze your feelings before talking about what's going on. I'm not saying there's anything wrong with that. I just ask that you not close the door on me. I have broad shoulders, lean on them, or hit them if that makes you feel better, but please don't shut me out," I stated.

"I'm going to need your help with that, Daniel. It's how I've always processed my feelings," Nicole openly shared her challenge.

Offering reassurance I answered, "Not a problem, I'm right by your side. If you're upset, and not ready to talk about it, just tell me that. I will give you the space you need. It's hard for me to see you hurting, and not have a clue what's going on, or how to help."

We took a shower together, then sat in the living room listening to music. It was so relaxing. I found an excuse to go to the kitchen, and returned with a single red rose, which was hidden in a vase in the pantry. She was surprised. I also gave her an envelope and said, "This is for my lady, the love of my life."

Her eyes lit up, and she gave me her million-dollar smile.

"I wrote this letter to you yesterday morning and meant to slide it under your front door. The guys made sure I didn't go near the house, so I saved it for today."

She opened the envelope and began reading:

Dear Nicole, I woke up this morning and the sun was shining brightly. I reached out for you and realized that you, the real sunshine of my life, weren't there. I smiled with the thought that this was our day, and the last day I would wake up without you next to me. You are an incredible lady, and I am so happy to have you as my life partner. I wanted to wait until today to tell you the song I chose for our first dance together. The song is called "We Both Deserve Each Other's Love," sung by Jeffrey Osborne. The timing is perfect for us. We were meant to be together. Thank you for accepting my heart, all my love, and especially thank you for accepting my name. Please take my hand and walk beside me. The best is yet to come. I love you.

"Daniel, that is so beautiful. I love you too. I'm glad you didn't give it to me yesterday, I would've been crying all day."

I reached out my hand, and she took it. We walked side by side to the bedroom. We sat on the chaise lounge chair in the bedroom and talked about our future together. I really liked the chair and decided I would buy one for my man cave. Nicole called it my man cave, but I figured she will probably spend more time there than I will.

"Honey, when we talked earlier, I told you what I needed from you. I'd like to hear what you need and want from me," I stated.

"The main thing I ask for is your patience. Since we started our relationship, I've been on a huge emotional roller coaster. I've never displayed so much emotion in my life. I feel like I'm crying all the time, and I know it's probably getting on your nerves," she said.

"Not at all, and I do understand what you mean. I was always the strong silent type of guy. No one ever knew what I was thinking or feeling. When I went to our support group meeting for the first time, I was really surprised to see other guys express themselves so openly. One week they announced we would be having two psychology interns speak to us. Your Dr. Holly was one of them, and Andrew was the other. It was their first time meeting each other. She was there to give us the female view on men and emotions," I responded, hoping to reassure her.

"Wow, it really is a small world."

"Yes, and quite an eye opener. She did some role playing with Andrew, and with us. Before then, I didn't realize it was ok to show emotions. Strong and silent is ok, but I learned that you women want us to communicate and show that we care, without you always having to ask. At first, it's hard to channel emotions, especially when they are so new to you. I understand your feeling, and don't worry, you're not getting on my nerves." I reached for her hand and gave it a squeeze.

"Good! Also, you've raised the bar high. You've charmed, and completely spoiled me. I'm expecting that to continue. It doesn't have to be big, or elaborate, but I just need to know you care, and that I'm special to you," she said with confidence.

"Not a problem. We will hold each other accountable. Now that I know what you need from me, tell me what you want," I teased.

Nicole gave me a sly smile, and said, "I want you to make love to me."

"You never have to ask for that. Of course, you could always rip off my clothes, and throw me on the bed, like you did last night," I said, having a hard time controlling my laughter. She opened her mouth in shock and was suddenly speechless. I could tell she was trying to think of a snappy retort, so I decided to take advantage of her silence. I smiled at her and said, "Don't look so shocked. I like it when you take charge like that. Come on, let's go to bed."

♡

Chapter 22

We've been back to reality for two weeks. I thought it would be a big adjustment for us, but everything is going well. Nicole gave me a "honey-do" list, which I knew was mostly to keep me busy and make me feel at home. She loved the remote-control sound system in the mountain cabin, so I set up a system for her. She loved pushing buttons to make music play in different parts of the house. She thought I was a genius, so I decided not to tell her the house was already wired for it.

We enjoyed decorating my man cave. I was surprised that Nicole really meant that to be my space. It was decorated in black, gray, and maroon. The maroon was her idea. According to her, it would make the room "pop". I had no idea what that meant, and decided I didn't want to know. It turned out, she was right. The maroon made a huge difference. I bought a black and gray chaise lounge chair to go with my black leather sofa and chair, which I brought over from my house. Nicole added maroon throw pillows, and a black, gray, and maroon area rug. The curtains were a blend of gray and maroon, with a little cream. My favorite thing was the picture collage she made. It contained pictures from trips we had taken together, and pictures from our favorite park. In the center of the collage, was a picture of us on our wedding day. The room was wide, so we arranged the furniture to make it look like it was two different spaces. I even had a half bath.

Joe and Elaine were coming over for dinner, and Nicole's spaghetti sauce had been simmering since early morning. It smelled so good. Just as my stomach was beginning to growl, she yelled upstairs to tell me lunch was ready. Lunch was a BLT sandwich and black bean soup. It was delicious. I'll admit, it took me a while to get used to turkey bacon, but I'm ok with it now. The bread was good too. Nicole told me it was sourdough bread. She went on to tell me sourdough bread had a higher level of vitamins, minerals, and antioxidants than other breads. I acted interested, but if it tasted good, I really didn't care about its make up.

"Daniel, I learned Dr. Holly and Andrew are both living in rental homes," Nicole said.

"How did you find this out, and what difference does it make to us?"

"You can find almost anything on the internet, and I was thinking maybe they would be interested in buying your home," she said.

"Oh, ok. That sounds like a good idea. Maybe you can

give her a call on Monday, or have you called her already?" I asked.

"No, I wanted to mention it to you first."

"Thank you, my little researcher," I responded, with pride.

"And thank you, for all of the work you've done around the house this week," Nicole said with gratitude.

"My pleasure. Would you like to come up to my place?" I asked.

I leaned forward to kiss her on the cheek and then added seducingly, "Have I told you today that I love you?"

"Yes, you have, and I'm happy to hear it again," she gushed.

"I love you honey. And before you ask, yes, I'm flirting with you,"

We smiled at each other, she turned the stove off, and I led her upstairs.

I turned the music on and started to dance with her. Her body felt so good next to mine. We danced to a few songs, then sat on the couch to cuddle. I held her face between my hands, and just looked at her and smiled. She really was the answer to my prayers. I kissed her, and, as my hands began to roam, I heard her moan. The couch was a sofa bed, and before things went too far, I thought I'd better pull the bed out.

"You are a beautiful, and incredibly sexy lady. I can't stop looking at you and touching your body," I said.

Nicole gave me her million-dollar smile, and said, "You have the same effect on me. I can't stop looking at your buff body either."

I unbuttoned her blouse and pulled it off. In slow motion, I pulled off the rest of her clothes. I saw her shiver and covered her with the sheet. She didn't need to worry; I would warm her up very quickly. I removed my clothes and began kissing her all over. I lingered on certain parts, mostly to tease her. She was moaning, and begging me to make love to her, so I did! I watched her face as I moved in a slow steady motion. I've never seen her look this sexy. I sped up, and she matched my moves. She felt so good. I made love to her until I felt her shiver, this time it wasn't from being cold. She moved on top and began working her magic on me. Her movements were sending me out of control. She ran her tongue across my nipple, and that threw me over the edge. I grabbed her butt to bring her body closer to mine. At that point, we both let loose. I heard her scream for more, and I gave her everything she asked for.

$\heartsuit$

Chapter 23

inner with Elaine and Joe was enjoyable. It's only been two weeks since we last saw them, but it seemed like forever. Daniel couldn't resist showing Joe his man cave, so Elaine and I spent time catching up, while eating dessert.

"You and Daniel are glowing; marriage certainly agrees with you. How was your trip to the mountains?"

"It was the perfect getaway. I've always enjoyed the quiet solitude of being in the mountains. Being there with Daniel was like the icing on the cake, "I said, with a big smile on my face.

Elaine interjected, "Speaking of cake, this is delicious. What kind of cake is it?"

"It's called Almost Heaven Cake. It's one of my favorite recipes. I made it for Daniel a few months ago, and he loved it. It was his idea to have it for dessert today."

"Well, you know Joe has a big, sweet tooth. You'll

have to give me the recipe," Elaine said, as she licked the fork.

"I will, and you can also take half of it home. Let's go see what they're doing, we may never get them away from Daniel's getaway."

We walked up the stairs and could hear Daniel and Joe laughing. The TV and music were playing, so I'm sure Daniel was showing off his new toys. I couldn't help but smile. Sometimes, they acted like teenage boys, and it was always amusing to see them together.

"Elaine, look at this space! I'm going to need my own man cave too," Joe exclaimed.

Elaine and I looked at each other and started laughing. "We have dessert downstairs for you," I teasingly said.

It seemed that the mention of food was the only thing that could distract them from their toys.

After eating dessert, we sat in the living room talking. Joe asked Daniel what he was planning to do with his home.

"Nicole and I were discussing that this morning. We will be selling it but haven't worked out the details yet."

Joe leaned forward and said, "I have a proposition for you. As you know, I've always loved that house. We had lunch with Holly and Andrew a few days ago, and they fell in love with our house. How do you feel about selling your home to Elaine and me?"

Daniel and I looked at each other in shock. We decided the six of us would get together and work out all the details. Holly and Andrew would need to get a loan, Joe and Elaine could pay in cash after their home sold.

"Nicole and I have a proposition for you as well. What are you doing for the holidays?" Daniel asked.

"We really haven't given it much thought," Joe responded.

"Would you like to come to Jamaica with us?" Daniel asked.

Joe and Elaine looked at each other, and Elaine spoke up first.

"We would love that," she said, with a smile.

"You still get your two weeks' stay that we gave you at our wedding. We thought it would be fun to explore the island with you," Daniel said with joy.

The evening ended on a happy note, and I packed leftovers for them to take home.

Chapter 24

I woke up at 5 a.m. the next morning. Daniel was sleeping soundly. I didn't want to disturb his rest, so I eased out of the bed. I sat in the living room with a cup of hot tea. Soft music played in the background, and the fireplace glowed. It felt and looked very cozy. It was the perfect atmosphere as I sat writing a note to Daniel. After a while, I heard him in the bathroom. I looked up when he came down the hallway and stood at the entrance to the living room.

"Honey, are you ok," he asked.

"Yes I am. I put coffee on for you. Why don't you grab a cup and join me," I offered.

We sat in silence while enjoying the music. I kissed him on the cheek and handed him the note I had written. I watched his face as he began to read:

"Dear Daniel, I woke up this morning with a feeling of

serenity. I watched you sleeping, and realized you are the main reason for my good feelings. I fell for you the first time we ran together in the park, and it scared me. I remember thinking how smooth and calm you were. You have brought out feelings and emotions in me that I never knew existed. You made me realize it's ok to be strong, but that I don't always have to be. Thank you for always being by my side, for your shoulders to lean on, and for being my rock. The giddy five-year- old in me is in love with you too. I am so happy to be your wife, and I will take good care of you. I look forward to the rest of our life together. Thank you for putting a big smile on my face. You found the light in me that I couldn't find. I will always love you."

Daniel looked at me in response to the letter, "This means the world to me. Thank you honey. Just for the record, when we first met, I wasn't being smooth and calm. My tongue was stuck to the roof of my mouth, and I couldn't think of anything to say. I remember admiring your ease as you talked."

I chuckled, and said, "Just to let you know, I wasn't talking with ease. Sometimes, when I get nervous, I can't stop talking. That's what happened that day,"

We had a good laugh at how we had misread each other that first day.

"I had to really think how I was going to get your attention. I thought you were a smart and sophisticated woman, and I knew that side of you wasn't going to let me in. You are very direct, and to the point. I figured that scared a lot of guys away. I was determined I wasn't going anywhere, and I wasn't planning to give up, either. One day, by accident, you let out your inner five-year- old. I knew she was the key to winning your heart. I put all my efforts into charming that side of you," Daniel confessed.

"Well, I'm glad you kept trying. Thank you for bringing out that part of me. It's nice not to be so serious all the time."

We hugged, and I could hear his stomach growling. I said, "Come on, I'll make breakfast for you,"

A few hours later, we pulled into the church parking lot, and one of the older church ladies parked next to us.

"There's Ms. Betsy, Daniel said. "I haven't seen her in a while. I went by her house to check on her and she wasn't home."

"Who is she?"

Daniel offered an explanation, "Her husband was pastor of the church when I first moved here to attend college. They used to invite me to dinner a lot. She's also your biggest fan, Nicole."

"Does she know me?" I asked.

He continued to explain, "No, the first time I took you to church with me, Ms. Betsy was sitting beside me. She whispered in my ear and asked if you were my girlfriend. I told her I wasn't sure yet, I was working on it. She told me to get my act together and work harder at it before someone else stole you from me."

"That's so cute," I said.

Daniel added, "She's a sweet lady. Her husband, Melvin, passed away years ago. They have three children who live in different states. Let's go help her out of the car."

"Ms. Betsy, where have you been," Daniel said, with a smile.

Ms. Betsy responded, "Daniel, come here and give me a hug! For the last few months, I've been visiting my children. They're trying to get me to move in with one of them."

I watched as they hugged, then Daniel took my hand and pulled me closer. That brought a big smile to Ms. Betsy's face. He smiled, and proudly said, "Ms. Betsy, I want to formally introduce you to Nicole, my wife. We were married a few weeks ago,"

"That is wonderful. Nicole, may I give you a hug," she asked.

"Of course, you can, I love hugs," I said.

Ms. Betsy whispered in my ear, but it really wasn't a whisper. She said, "Daniel is a keeper, be sure to take good care of him."

I could tell Daniel heard what she said. He smiled, wrapped his arms around both of us, and we walked into the church. We sat behind Joe and Elaine. Daniel leaned forward to whisper to them, and they both nodded.

"Ms. Betsy, would you like to go out to lunch with us after church? We will follow you home, you can leave your car, and ride with Nicole and me to the restaurant," Daniel asked.

The big smile on her face told us her answer. He winked at me, and made me smile, as well.

Pastor Bill walked in, and we were captivated for the next hour.

Lunch turned out to be a little party. Bill and Cheryl

joined us. Ms. Betsy giggled like a little girl the entire time. I was so glad Daniel thought to have this impromptu get together.

We drove Ms. Betsy home and sat in the car talking. She leaned forward, and said, "Daniel, I have something to tell you. I've decided to live with my son in Maryland and will be moving within the next month. I've been thinking about the move for a while but wanted to make sure you were happy first."

I glanced at Daniel and noticed a look of sadness on his face. He took her hand and said, "Ms. Betsy, I'm happy for you, and a little sad too. You were like a second mother to me throughout my college years. When my mom passed away while I was in graduate school, you and your family took me under your protective wings and helped me get through that difficult time. You can count on Nicole and me to assist you with your move, and help you get settled in Maryland."

The three of us held hands, as we walked her to the front door.

Chapter 25

Nicole called Katelyn, her realtor, and they worked together on the best way to sell Joe's house and mine. We knew we didn't want to put them on the market. Katelyn and Nicole agreed on something called a For Sale by Owner. Once it was explained to us, it sounded like the best route to take. We all got together, agreed on the terms, and signed documents. Holly and Andrew had already been working with a lender and making a lot of progress. It looked like they would be able to close on Joe's house within 30 days. We decided to have the closings a day apart in case there were any delays. Once we were certain Holly and Andrew's loan would proceed, Joe could start moving into my house. Elaine was so excited and was bombarding Joe with decorating ideas. It was fun watching him squirm for a change.

Nicole surprised me and met me for lunch after my morning classes. We ate cafeteria food, but I didn't mind.

Her being there made my day. I told her, "Honey, I'd like to have a date with you Saturday evening,"

"A date, you mean like going out to dinner, "she asked.

"Yeah, dinner will be included, but I'm not just talking about a night out for dinner. This will be a special evening."

She was looking confused, so I thought I'd better explain.

"You told me that I had raised the bar very high, and that you expected me to continue the way I treated you when I was wooing you. That is what I'm trying to do."

"Ahhh! I would love a date with you," Nicole gushed.

"You've raised the bar high too, and I have expectations as well. I would like you to wear a dress on our date. You look great in everything you wear, but I love it when you wear dresses. Maybe I'll take you dancing after dinner," I said in a flirtatious way.

"That's an easy request to fulfill. I'm looking forward to our date," she said.

I walked her to the car, then went back to prepare for my afternoon class. That was easier than I expected. I can't wait for her to see the real reason I asked her for a date.

The rest of the week flew by. Saturday was a beautiful day, with temps expected in the 70's. The joys of southern living in the fall, you never know what to expect with the weather. I was looking forward to this evening. Nicole had been very secretive the last few days, but I could tell she was excited about preparing for our date. She said I couldn't see her outfit until tonight, so I decided to be patient and work on my own attire.

Nicole looked beautiful! She had on a dress that was royal blue at the top, and black at the bottom. The top flared slightly, making the bottom look slender. It fit her shape perfectly. She wore a black onyx necklace, with earrings to match. She even wore heels.

I couldn't help smiling when she told me how handsome I looked. I decided I would change my tie and wear a blue one, to match her outfit. We are a good-looking couple.

I turned the music on in the car, and the first song that played was "We're Going All the Way."

"Daniel, I love that song. Jeffrey Osborne sings it. Elaine told me he's coming to town next week. Did you know that," she asked with amazement.

"Next week? No, I didn't know that," I said, with a smirk on my face.

We pulled into the parking lot of the restaurant. I was told it was the perfect place for a date night, and it lived up to its reputation. The food was delicious, and the room was nice. There were booths instead of open tables, which gave a sense of privacy and coziness. There was a gas log fireplace in the corner, which was mostly for looks and atmosphere.

"Daniel, this is a wonderful place, I can't wait to tell Elaine and Joe about it," she said, with her cute, giddy, five-year-old look.

"It's definitely a winner. We will have to come again. I'm also enjoying looking at your beautiful body. You look very sexy tonight," I added, obviously flirting with her.

"Are you still using your charm on me," she asked, as she lowered her eyes in a seductive manner.

"Nah, I'm being totally honest. That dress fits you so well. The night is still young, are you ready to go?"

I turned the music on in the car, and another Jeffrey Osborne song started to play. It was called "You Should Be Mine."

"That's another nice song. Did you know he calls it the Woo Woo song?"

"Didn't know that. What does that mean?" I was having a hard time keeping a straight face.

"I'm not sure, but, at concerts, he often invites the audience to sing the Woo Woo part. Sometimes he takes off his suit jacket. He's in great physical shape."

"Nicole, I can't believe you said that! Look at me! He doesn't look nearly as good as I do!"

Nicole smiled and responded, "You're cute when you act jealous, but there is no need to be. He's a figure on the screen. You're real, my everything, my boo. You're my first thought every morning and my last thought every night."

"Great job of sugarcoating, honey," I said.

She had the nerve to smile and bat her eyes at me.

"I'm not sure this is the right time to tell you, but Elaine was wrong. Jeffrey's not coming next week, he's in town now. We're headed to his concert. Joe took Elaine to dinner and should be telling her about now. We decided to tell you at the same time, so you wouldn't have a chance to talk with each other about it before the time was right," I said, with difficulty controlling my smile.

"Oh, my goodness, Daniel, what a nice surprise. Thank you," she responded, with an open-mouthed look of awe.

"You're welcome. I'm not jealous, but if you start drooling when he takes his jacket off, you may have to get an Uber home," I said.

Shortly after, we pulled into the parking lot of the event center. We met up with Joe and Elaine and took our seats in the VIP section of the front row. I was enjoying the look on Nicole's face. I also thought it was cute that she thought I was jealous. That would give me a lot of brownie points for later, and I was adding them up without shame.

It was a great concert. The Woo Woo song came on, and Jeffrey removed his jacket. Nicole smiled at me and gave me a kiss on the cheek. She held my hand as Jeffrey sang.

The concert was nearing the end, and Jeffrey started to speak.

"This is my last song. Bear with me while I tell you a story. Many years ago, I gave a concert here for homecoming. I arrived a few days early and decided to go to the campus gym to work out. There were a lot of young ladies in the gym, and naturally, I thought they were there because I was in town. It was a big blow to my ego when I realized they weren't there for me, they were trying to get the attention of the guy working in the gym that day. Suddenly, none of the ladies could get their machines to work and kept calling the guy over for help. He took it in stride and gave them tips on how to work the equipment. I must admit, I felt some kind of way, not getting the ladies' attention. I sat down to talk with him at the end of his shift, and realized he was a nice guy. We kept in touch over the years. He told me that he recently got married, and that my song, 'We Both Deserve Each Other's Love,' was his song to his new wife. So, I'm dedicating this song to my buddy, Daniel, and his wife, Nicole."

Jeffrey started to sing. Nicole was in total shock. I wrapped my arms around her and kissed her. As I looked up, I noticed we were on the monitor for everyone to see. I kissed her again, and held her close to me, as Jeffrey sang.

Chapter 26

I couldn't stop smiling on the way home from the concert. Daniel always amazes me with his surprises. Usually, I can tell when he's up to something, but this time he caught me totally off guard. I can't believe Elaine got the dates mixed up!

"Daniel, I enjoyed our date. Thank you for taking me to the concert. How do you get so many people to help you surprise me? It seems like you know everyone," I said, while still floating on Cloud Nine.

"Over the years, I've met a lot of people. I've always tried to be a nice guy and lend a hand whenever it was needed. I didn't know how important that was, until I went through my divorce. I didn't really talk about it, but I seemed to get smiles and encouragement from all over. As much as Joe and my frat brothers tease me, they are very happy that I have you in my life. They are my biggest supporters, and I owe them all so much. There are many people looking out for me and rooting for us. It feels so good," he replied, in a matter-of-fact way.

I confirmed, "Yes, it does. I thought it was so sweet that Ms. Betsy put her move on hold to make sure you were happy. You're a great guy. I'm so happy to be in your life."

As we were pulling into the driveway, he remarked, "I can't begin to tell you how happy I am to have you in my life as well. Come upstairs to my place, and we can relax and talk more."

We changed our clothes and walked upstairs. Daniel turned the music on, and the song "We Both Deserve Each Other's Love" began to play. He wrapped his arms around me, and we began a slow, sensuous dance. The song ended, and we gazed into each other's eyes. We kissed, he took my hand, and led me to the chaise to sit. I scooted close to him, and he wrapped his arms around me.

"Nicole," he said, "the main reason I love to surprise you, is because of your reactions. You get so excited, and it doesn't matter whether it's a small surprise, or a big one, like tonight. You encourage me to be the best I can be, and to always do my best for you."

I couldn't stop smiling. "I love you, Daniel. You are the best thing that ever happened to me."

"I think we can agree that we are the best for each other. It seems like God made us go through a lot of trials so we could be ready for each other. When we first met at the fundraiser, I was a broken man. I wasn't trying to pick you up when I offered to walk you to your car, I was just trying to be a gentleman. Over the years, I worked very hard to put the pieces of my broken life back to-gether, and to become whole again. It seems like you were doing the same thing," Daniel stated.

I agreed, "Yes, I was. It seemed to take forever be-cause I had pushed my feelings aside for so long. When I look back, I can see tremendous growth in myself. I'm glad we didn't try to get together when we were both in that bad state."

"I'm glad too. It seems our timing, or I should say, God's timing was perfect. By the time I met you in the park the first time, my life seemed to be getting back on track. The only piece missing was my heart. It was in place but felt empty. The more time we spent together, the more my heart began to fill, and overflow with love for you. I had been praying for a second chance to get love right, and you are it. I love what we are building to-gether. I love how each of us has grown personally, and I especially love the growth we've brought to our relation-ship with each other. So, I will continue to surprise you, and to love you like you've never been loved before," Daniel offered me reassurance.

I looked up at him, and knew my face was beaming.

"I love seeing that smile on your face. The best thing about us is that our relationship is not one-sided. You're much more reserved and controlled than I am, but I've never once questioned or doubted your feelings for me. You love me with a fierceness that blows my mind. Your actions are so quiet and subtle, yet so very apparent to most people we meet. I love the way you love me," he said, as he pulled me closer and held me in his arms.

Chapter 27

I sat in my jail cell, feeling lonely, and so stupid. I can't believe I fell for Charles Maxwell's stupid, harebrained idea. According to my attorney, the one thing in my favor was that the gun I had was unloaded. It was a minor technicality, but one that could possibly reduce my sentence. He also thought a plea bargain was worth thinking about.

My friend Cathy came by to see me today. She showed me pictures of Daniel and Nicole at a concert last weekend. According to her, the pictures went viral, and were all over social media. I've never seen Daniel look so happy, or so much in love. It really hurt, but I know losing him was my own fault.

I guess I didn't realize that Daniel and I had a good marriage. He was very romantic and loving, but I thought that was boring. He worked a lot, and I just wanted to have fun. He kept telling me he was working hard to secure our future. I had several counseling sessions after coming to jail. At first, I used them as a way of possibly making my time here shorter, but as time went on, I found them helpful. For a long time, I blamed Daniel for the breakup of our marriage. That thought was selfish. Daniel was a good husband, and I quickly found out when he's done, that's it. We never had a conversation after he caught me in bed with Tom.

One day when I was visiting Cathy, I saw Daniel's car parked down the street. I was very curious, so I started visiting more often, and kept seeing his car there. The first time I saw Nicole, I kept thinking she looked familiar. It took a while before I remembered she was Charles' ex-wife. I met her a few times when I worked for him, and thought she was very stiff. It was hard to imagine what Daniel saw in her. She didn't seem like his type at all. I became obsessed with her and started following her. I saw her and Daniel running in the park a few times. He always tried to get me to run with him, but I wasn't interested. I was not about to sweat, or get my hair messed up. One day Cathy and I were walking in the neighborhood and saw Daniel and Nicole washing the car. They seemed to be having fun. Nicole aimed the hose at Daniel and kept spraying him. He chased her around the yard, and finally grabbed the hose from her. I thought he was going to hose her down. Instead, he dropped it on the ground, grabbed her, and kissed her. She was laughing like a little kid, and he kept kissing her. I couldn't believe they were acting like that in public. Cathy and I decided the next time we saw Nicole alone; we would tell her Daniel and I were reuniting. That should put a wedge between them, and maybe give me time to make a move on Daniel. After all, I got him to fall for me once, it shouldn't be too hard to get him to fall for me again. Tom had asked for a divorce, and I felt completely lost and alone.

Boy, was I wrong. I must admit, the day Cathy and I told Nicole I was going back to Daniel, she showed a lot of class. Her phone rang, and I could see Daniel's picture on the screen. I thought that was corny, but to each his own. She excused herself and walked into the house. Later that evening, I saw Daniel's car in the driveway. After a while, I saw him get in the car, and thought he was leaving. He was pulling his car into the garage. There went my opportunity.

I was about to give up, until the day I ran into Charles. At first his crazy scheme sounded like a good idea. He had me keeping an eye on Nicole, and he was doing the same with his soon-to-be ex-wife, Lily. I found out he was planning to kill Daniel and Lily. Thankfully she outsmarted him.

Once I discovered what his real plan was, I removed the bullets from the gun he had given me. I was afraid to back out because I thought he would kill me too. I was standing at my assigned spot in the park when I heard a gunshot. I was going to get back in the car and drive down the trail when I saw Nicole running in the direction of the sound. I held the gun on her to delay her getting to Daniel before I could. Before I could blink, she jumped on me, pushing me to the ground. I saw the ring on her left hand and tried to punch her in the face. She beat the crap out of me. I really underestimated her. I'm still sore, and my jaw and broken ribs are healing at last. Thankfully, I didn't need surgery for my ruptured spleen. I thought of bringing assault charges against her, but my attorney highly discouraged it.

I've had a lot of time to think in the last few months. I was stupid and selfish. I'm happy for Daniel, and glad he found a woman who seems to give him everything I didn't. The one bright spot in all this drama is that Tom and I are talking again. He came to see me a few times and put the divorce on hold for the moment. Maybe there's hope for me after all.

Chapter 28

Nicole and I have had a busy few weeks. We were so blessed this year and decided to sponsor five families for Christmas. Shopping for gifts was rewarding, but boy were we tired. I'm looking forward to playing Santa again this year. We will have the party and gift exchange in two weeks. I'm trying to get Nicole to play Mrs. Claus, but no luck with that so far.

We also helped Ms. Betsy get packed and moved to Maryland. Her son flew down and rented a truck to move her things. Ms. Betsy rode with Nicole and me in the car. I felt sad leaving her in Maryland, but I know it was the best choice for her. Her son's house has a finished basement, which will be her new home. She will have her privacy and have someone close by to look out for her. She made a photo album for Nicole and me. It had pictures of me in my younger days. They brought back so many memories for me. At the end of the album, was a picture of the three of us together. Ms. Betsy wanted to make sure we didn't forget her. There wasn't a chance of that happening because she was a major part of my life for many years.

Thanksgiving is next week. Holly and Andrew will close on their house on Monday, Joe and Elaine will close on my house on Tuesday. I let them move in two weeks ago. I hear Elaine is having a ball decorating. They invited us over for Thanksgiving dinner. It will be interesting to see how the house looks with new owners. I thought I would miss living there but haven't given it a second thought since moving in with Nicole.

It was a lazy Saturday. I made breakfast, and shortly after eating, we went back to bed. Nicole was sleeping and I couldn't resist touching her. I kissed her on the neck and shoulders, and slowly traveled down her body. I heard her moan and pulled her closer. I whispered, "Wake up sleeping beauty, your prince is here."

She opened her eyes and had a big smile on her face. She said, "Daniel, I was dreaming about you."

"Mmmm, let's see if I can make your dreams come true," I said with a mischievous grin.

"You already have. I'm all yours, have your way with me," she responded, with a sexy tone.

I began kissing her breasts. I could feel her breathing change as I took her right breast in my mouth. She started squirming, but I wasn't going to let go. My fingers roamed down her body and played with other parts. I licked and sucked on her right breast, then moved to the left one. I let go of her breast and gave her a sloppy kiss on the mouth. I watched her face as my fingers contin-ued to tease her. She had a dreamy look on her face. I took her right breast in my mouth again. When I felt she couldn't take any more teasing, I slowly entered her. She wrapped her legs around me, and we began moving to-gether. I licked her left breast and could feel her beginning to lose control. She was moaning and scream-ing my name. I started moving faster and deeper. I made love to her until we were both satisfied. I pulled her in my arms and kissed her. She leaned her head on my chest, and we both fell asleep.

I woke a few hours later to find Nicole smiling at me.

"Hey sleepy head, are you ready for some lunch," she asked.

"Sure, I'll make lunch," I volunteered.

"You cooked breakfast, now it's my turn," Nicole in-sisted.

I denied her request, "This is my day to pamper you. Give me a few minutes, and I'll meet you in the kitchen."

"What can I do to help," she asked.

"Nothing, just sit still and talk with me while I cook."

I put some chicken wings and potato wedges in the air fryer. While they were cooking, I made a salad. We sat down to eat, and Nicole kept licking her lips. I had a feeling it wasn't because of the chicken wings. I had on sweatpants and a sleeveless t-shirt, to show off my biceps. She couldn't stop looking at me.

"You're becoming quite a chef, and you're cute, too," she said, with a seductive smile.

I just smiled. I loved it when she flirted with me.

"What's for dessert?" she asked.

"That's a surprise, you have to clean your plate first," I responded with a smile.

I loved teasing her, so I changed the subject.

"Are you ready to decorate for Christmas?" I asked.

"I haven't thought much about it since we will be in Jamaica," she answered.

"I don't want to disappoint the giddy five-year-old in you. We should at least put up a tree. If we do it next weekend, we'll have time to enjoy it," I stated.

"Sounds good. It's nice of you to think of my inner five-year-old," she said.

"The tree is for her; dessert is for you. Maybe I'll put on my Santa hat and let you sit on my lap," I teased.

After lunch, I turned the music and fireplace on, and we sat in the living room talking. She "accidentally" touched my arms several times. She couldn't keep her eyes off me. It's shameful, but I was really enjoying teasing her. I held her face in my hands and gave her a long, sensual kiss. She was about to melt, so I suggested we take a shower together.

I poured shower gel in my hands and began massaging her shoulders and back. I turned her around and started kissing her breast. She was floating, and I let my fingers roam all over her body. She was having a hard time maintaining her usual control, and I just kept playing with her.

"Daniel, why do you keep teasing me," she demanded.

I tried to look as innocent as possible. I responded, "Teasing you? You told me this morning you were all mine, and I could have my way with you."

"THAT WAS JUST FOR THIS MORNING," she said with a glare.

"Ohhh, I thought it was a one-day pass. My bad!" I licked my lips and smiled at her. She narrowed her eyes and scowled at me. She was so cute when she tried to look tough.

I grabbed her butt and pulled her close to me. My lips were roaming all over her body. She shivered, and I offered to wrap my arms around her, to protect her from the cold. She didn't answer, so I put my mouth over her breast and acted like a suckling infant. My hands continued to roam. I turned the water off, grabbed a towel, and offered to help her dry off. I was all thumbs and kept "accidentally" touching her in certain places.

She looked like she was on fire. I lifted her in my arms and carried her to the bed. My body covered hers, and I started kissing and caressing her. She was moaning and squirming. Finally, I gave her what I knew she wanted. Damn, she felt so good, I didn't want to stop. I made love to her until we were both exhausted. She smiled at me, and I know I had a big smile on my face as well. I pulled her in my arms and held her tightly. I didn't want to let her go. I wondered if she still wanted dessert.

Chapter 29

Thanksgiving morning was chilly, but the sun was shining brightly. We had a quick five-mile run, then headed home to prepare for Thanksgiving dinner. I made lunch while Nicole made banana pudding for dessert. I was looking forward to dinner at Joe's. Bill and Cheryl would be there too, so it would feel like old times.

It felt weird pulling into the driveway of my old house. It felt even weirder ringing the doorbell, instead of using my key to get in. Nicole reached for my hand and gave it a squeeze. She kissed me on the cheek, and at that moment, Joe opened the door.

"Geez, man, get a room," Joe joked.

He kept laughing. He was quite a comedian at times.

Elaine had done a beautiful job of decorating for the holidays. When I noticed Nicole's reaction, I was glad I had encouraged her to put up a tree, even though we wouldn't be home for Christmas.

The ladies went to the kitchen, and we guys went to the den to watch football. The room was decorated in purple and gold, our frat colors. They had done a good job of making the house feel like a home.

Although Bill was more subtle than Joe, he also enjoyed joking at my expense. I took it all in stride and knew I would get them both back.

"You and Nicole are still glowing like neon lights. Marriage must be agreeing with you. Have you had your first argument yet," Bill asked.

"We've had disagreements, but not real arguments. In the beginning of our relationship, we talked about settling differences before the day's end. It works for us," I said.

Bill asked how we've managed to make that work.

I answered, "I promised her I would always end each day on a positive note. There's only been a few times when that was a challenge, but I still did it. Carrying things into the next day seems to make them appear worse than they really are. I know how stubborn we both can be, and Nicole really isn't a person you want to argue with. So, I send her a text every night, and she sends me one every morning."

"That seems so simple," Bill responded.

"Sometimes it is, sometimes it's not. Overall, I have no complaints. She loves me and takes great care of me. I do the same for her," I said, with a smile.

"What do you think is the biggest key to your successful marriage," Bill inquired further.

I thought for a moment and replied, "Hmm, I guess the biggest thing was learning to choose my battles carefully.

I'm pretty easy going and I really don't like to argue, so I give in most of the time. On the other hand, Nicole knows when to back away and let me lead. I still take her on dates, and I love surprising her. We still flirt with each other. I send her flowers, and we write love notes to each other. Every evening we like to relax and listen to music. Sometimes we talk, sometimes we just sit still and enjoy each other's company."

"Thanks buddy! I'm asking so many questions for two reasons. I'm writing a book about relationships, how to make them work, and how to maintain the spark, no matter how old you are, or how long you've been together. The second reason is, we've been thinking about making a few changes in our male support group," he said.

"That's great news about the book, Bill. What kind of changes will you be making with the group?" I asked.

Bill answered, "We're still working on that. The group has been very helpful and successful, but maybe it's time to add a bit of flavor to it. We think it will be good to have ladies at some of the meetings. I'd appreciate any input you may have."

"If you want great input, there are three ladies in the kitchen. Women are the greatest initiators of change. Speaking of them, I'm hungry, let's see if dinner's ready," I said.

Joe laughed at that and said, "Not much has changed with you, brother, you're always hungry. Let's go eat. I'm looking forward to Nicole's banana pudding."

We all held hands while Bill blessed the food. Afterwards, we each said one thing we were thankful for. As we began to eat, I smiled and winked at Nicole. Unfortunately, the others saw it. Darn, now Joe had one more thing to tease me about.

Dinner was wonderful. Since the ladies did all the cooking, Joe, Bill, and I volunteered to cleanup. The ladies went to the den to watch football.

"Joe," I said, "The house looks great, you and Elaine have done a wonderful job."

"Thanks, the one thing I really want is a sound system like you have. I like the idea of having music playing throughout the house with a push of a button."

"That's easy to do," I said, "if you're free this weekend, I can come over and set it up for you. It should only take a few hours."

We walked down the hall toward the den and heard the ladies yelling at the TV. As we got to the door, we could hear Cheryl saying, "I can't believe he dropped that ball!"

I knew it was going to be a tough game, Elaine and Nicole were rooting for one team, while Cheryl was rooting for the other. Bill, Joe, and I looked at each other, uncertain if we wanted to enter the room. Thank goodness it was the end of the fourth quarter.

The game ended, and Nicole and Elaine were smugly happy. We ate dessert, and it was soon time for us all to head home. Elaine insisted we take leftovers home and gave us enough food to last a few days. It had been an enjoyable day with friends.

Later that evening, Nicole and I relaxed in front of the fireplace. The sound of soothing jazz played in the background. I laid on the sofa with my head on her lap.

She massaged my scalp and shoulders. I could feel myself drifting and went with the feeling.

I woke up an hour later. Nicole was sitting in the chair across from me, writing in a notebook. She looked up when she heard me yawn. She said, "Hey sleepy head, did you have a good nap?"

"I can't believe I fell asleep. I think your massage did it for me. Now I'm hungry, would you like a snack," I asked.

"I'll make turkey sandwiches. Plus, I made an extra banana pudding just for you. Do you want some," she asked.

"Yeah! I'll join you in the kitchen," I said, licking my lips in anticipation.

"I'll bring the food in here. I'm enjoying the cozy feeling of this room. Would you get the trays, they're in the hall closet."

After eating, and cleaning up, we settled on the couch again.

"You were looking very serious when I woke up. What are you writing about," I asked.

"Just random notes. When Bill talked about his book, it gave me a lot to think about. He said he wanted to interview me, so I'm trying to prepare as well as I can. When I think back over the last year or so, I'm amazed at how far we've come. Or, maybe how far I've come, is a better assessment," she responded.

Nicole rarely talks about feelings, and I wanted her to have her moment without my interruption. I simply nodded for her to go on.

"When I moved back here from Atlanta, I had a lot of things to think about. I had recently retired, but I knew I was too young to sit still and do nothing. Plus, that's just not my style. I kept praying for guidance, or maybe a bolt of lightning to drop and lead me in the right direction. When I didn't get the instant results I wanted, I decided to go for a run. Running usually gives me a kind of freedom from over-thinking everything. That was the day I first saw you in the park. At first, I thought maybe you were that bolt of lightning I was praying for. Then, I remembered the reason I came to the park was to clear my mind and stop thinking so much. Running with you was a bit unnerving. I was able to keep up, but the barrage of thoughts that usually filled my mind was replaced with feelings. This was completely foreign to me. I tried to push them away by running faster. That didn't work! Part of me wanted to stand still and hug you, the other part of me wanted to run as fast as I could in the opposite direction," she paused while recollecting her thoughts then continued.

"I couldn't stop looking at you the first time you came over to help me with my curtain rods, and to hang pictures. I had already planned to have someone come over and do it, but when you offered, I couldn't refuse. I also thought seeing you again would help me to stop thinking about you so much. Well, I was wrong about that too! I remember wishing I had studied psychology instead of architecture. My mind was playing all kinds of tricks on me, and I felt like I didn't have any control over my thoughts or emotions."

"The more time we spent together, the more I began to relax, and accept your presence in my life. I was feeling less afraid but was still nervous because you showed your emotions. You didn't just tell me how you felt, you showed me. After working so long in a male dominant architectural world, I wasn't used to displays of emotions. I finally realized you were not playing games, that you were for real. Your emotions didn't take away from your masculinity, in fact, they enhanced it. I was beginning to show more emotion by then, too. It wasn't as hard as I thought it would be, but I was still taking baby steps. I realized I was in love with you, and it didn't frighten me anymore. I wasn't good at saying the words, so I was hoping you could tell by my actions," she paused, and smiled shyly at me.

"When I woke up this morning, you were sleeping soundly. I watched you sleep, and it made me smile to know that you are my biggest blessing, not just on Thanksgiving, but every day. That day when I was praying for guidance, God was already working on it. He literally handed you to me on a silver platter. I'm glad I stopped fighting my feelings."

"I'm so thankful for you, and for us. You keep telling me the best is yet to come, but I say the best is already here. Thank you for loving me so well, and for showing me how to love you, the way you deserve to be loved. My heart has completely melted into yours. We are one! I'm so much in love with you, Daniel."

"Wow," was all I could say. There was no need for any other words. I kissed her and held her close to me. I held her in my arms all night. I don't think I've ever slept so soundly.

Chapter 30

I was busy getting dinner together when my phone buzzed. I knew it wasn't Daniel, he had just called to see if I needed him to pick up anything on his way home from class. I didn't recognize the number, so I decided to just answer and get rid of them quickly. It was Jeff Sinclair, Charles' attorney. He said Charles would like to meet with me, and asked if I could meet tomorrow morning. Daniel walked in just as I was telling Jeff I wanted to talk it over with my husband and would call him back within the hour.

"What do you need to talk over with me," Daniel asked, as he placed his briefcase on the chair.

"That was Charles' attorney. He asked if I would meet with Charles in the morning."

"How do you feel about that," he asked.

"I'm curious, otherwise I don't have any feelings about it at all."

"You should go. I'll go with you," he said, with a reassuring tone.

I called Jeff back and confirmed our meeting for 11:00 tomorrow.

The next morning, I felt very restless. I decided to get up and fix breakfast. That would at least keep me busy.

"Honey, do you want to go for a quick run before we eat," Daniel asked, with a concerned look.

"No, I really don't want to be that relaxed. Does that make sense?" I responded.

"Yes, it does, running relaxes you, and you don't want to be so at ease that you let your guard down with Charles," he said, as he took my hand in his.

We ate breakfast, showered, and prepared to leave. When we got there, I was told to leave my purse and cell phone outside with Daniel. He squeezed my hand, and I could feel his strength go through me. I was ready for this. After all, it would only be thirty minutes out of my day. Jeff was there and went to the other end of the room as I sat in the cubicle in front of Charles.

"Thank you for coming, Nicole, you look very nice," Charles said, with confidence.

Since I wasn't there for small talk, I didn't say anything. He got the message and began to explain the reason for the visit. He said, "I'll be detained for a while and am getting my business affairs together. You still have one-third ownership in the business, and I need your input."

"What do you mean I still have ownership? You gave me a settlement when we were divorced," I questioned, clearly in a state of shock.

"That was from your share of stock in the business. I wasn't sure what to do with the other part, so I left it alone. My partner, Kenneth, is ready to move forward. We can do it in several different ways. I can give you my third, which will give you two-thirds ownership, and make you the primary decision maker. I can sell my third to Kenneth, which would make him the primary. Legally, I can't do anything with your one-third unless you give me permission in writing. The business has been very profitable, and your portion is worth $3,000,000," he continued, in a monotone.

I tried not to look stunned as he delivered this news.

"What about your wife and son? It seems they should be getting part of the business," I stated.

"Lily will be getting a divorce settlement. She didn't play a part in making my business what it is, so she can't touch it, or the profits from it. Charles Jr. really isn't my son, so he will not profit from my business either. Since it isn't his fault that his mother is a strumpet, I'm not leaving him out. I set up a portfolio for him at birth when I thought he was my son. It is doing well, and with continued growth, he will be set for life. I don't want to put pressure on you, but I need an answer soon. I would like to go forward early next year. My trial is set for the end of February, and I'd like to have this behind me before then," he said, with authority.

"I can tell you for sure, that I don't want your portion of the business, nor do I want a hand in running it. Before I make any more decisions, I would like a profit and loss statement from your accountants, among other things. I'll give Jeff a list of what I want," I responded, with what I hope sounded confident.

"Now that's the Nicole I'm used to! I'll make sure you have everything you ask for. Thank you for coming," he said, and stood up, as a signal that our meeting was over.

I stood to leave, and he held his hand up.

"On a more serious note, Nicole, I know it doesn't mean anything to you now, but I would like to apologize for all of the hurt and pain I caused. I've had a lot of time to think lately, and I want to kick myself for the way I handled things in our marriage. I'm very proud of the way you picked yourself up, and moved forward, with the grace that you've always had in abundance. I can't talk with him now, but when the trial is over, I would like to apologize to your husband as well. He's a lucky man, and he put a glow on your face that I was never able to," he continued with obvious regret.

I turned, walked towards the door, and never looked back. Daniel stood up when I walked into the lobby.

He reached for my hand, and said, "Honey, are you ok? Do you want to talk about your visit with Charles?"

"All of a sudden, I'm starving. Can we go have lunch? I'll give you all the details of my talk with Charles," I responded, with a smile to reassure him I was ok.

"Of course. Let's run by The Burger Barn. It's a nice day, we can go to the park and eat at one of the shelters," he replied, with a visible sigh of relief.

We ate, and I told him everything Charles had said. His face showed he was just as shocked as I was when I first heard it.

"I'll meet with Jeff later this week, after he has all the documents I asked for. I want to set up an LLC. The money feels dirty, and I don't want it in our personal accounts. It's better to wait until the first of the year to transfer everything, for tax purposes, and because I don't want to be thinking about it as we prepare for our holiday. I intend to put the money to use by helping more with the Food Bank, and other charities. We will be able to help more families all year, and not just at the holidays," I said.

"I'm proud of you, honey. Let's go home," Daniel said.

Chapter 31

A few days later, I was busy making breakfast while Daniel showered. It took him a while to get used to eating a hot breakfast, he was used to making smoothies. It was also a good way for us to connect before going off to our busy days.

"Daniel, I have a confession to make," I said, with a timid smile.

"Ok, should I sit down for this," Daniel asked, with a confused look.

"Maybe you should," I responded.

He had a quizzical look on his face, and I didn't want to keep him in suspense any longer. I said, "I got an email from Linda, at the Food Bank this morning. She said the elves for the Christmas party have backed out, and Santa doesn't have any helpers. I was in a devilish mood when I responded, so I gave her Joe and Bill's phone numbers. She's calling them later today to thank them for being able to help at the last minute."

He burst out laughing, which was a great relief.

"You're not mad at me for doing that," I asked.

"Heck no, you just made my day. I would love to be a fly on the wall when they get the call. I wish I had thought of that, but it's funny coming from you. They have both earned that," he said, with a laugh.

"By the way, good luck with your meeting with Jeff Sinclair. Please text me when it's over so I know you're ok."

"I'll do even better than that, I'll drop by and have lunch with you," I promised.

"That's perfect. With exams next week, it's been slow the last few days. Love you honey, and I'll see you later." He gave me a kiss and headed out the door.

Jeff and I met a few hours later. He had also invited Dennis, the chief accountant. I was surprised and impressed that they had all the documents I requested. I had also asked Jeff to find out what happened to my profits from the last seven years. They were more honest and helpful than I knew I could ever expect from Charles.

Dennis started the conversation, without preamble. "Nicole, Charles started a miscellaneous account seven years ago. When I asked what it was for, he always said it was for incidentals. The account was in a different bank than our other accounts. Charles added to it once a year, and paid taxes on it. When you sent Jeff the list of documents you wanted to view, I paid a visit to Charles to get more information. It turns out, the so-called incidental account are your profits for the last seven years, with interest. I went back over all our accounts with more detail, and discovered the amount Charles deposited yearly in the account matched the same amount of profit he and Kenneth shared. He told me he started it as a separate, remote account just in case anything ever happened to the business. He also said he had hurt you deeply, so he set it aside so you would always have a secure financial future. As of day's end, yesterday, the amount in that account is $2,765,326.77. If you decide to sell your share of the business to Kenneth, you will gain an additional $3,289,888.47. The numbers may change slightly in the next few weeks, but it won't be a significant amount. I know this is a lot to throw at you, and I thank you for your patience, and for your thoroughness. Do you have any questions?"

"Thank you, Dennis. I really appreciate you getting this all together in a few days. I'm working with my attorney on the best type of account to put the money into. Everything should be set up no later than the second week of January. He will be calling Jeff and you if he needs anything else," I said.

"It was my pleasure, Nicole. By the way, you're a very thorough researcher. Let me know if you're ever looking for a second career," he chuckled.

We all laughed at that. I thanked them both again and headed out of the building. My head was spinning with all this information. Charles was quite a piece of work!

I picked up lunch and headed to the campus to meet Daniel. Since it was a beautiful day, we ate outside.

When we finished eating, I told him about my visit with Jeff and Dennis.

"I'm not sure what to think of Charles, and the way he handled all of this. Does this give you some sense of closure?" Daniel asked.

"I closed that book a long time ago, and never looked back. It's just like him to cause pain, and throw money at it, like the money is some type of healing balm," I said.

I noticed Daniel looking at me and asked what was wrong.

"I just had a thought. Is that why you insisted that our holiday gift to each other last year be non-monetary," he asked.

"You know, I never thought about it that way. Now that you mention it, I think you're right. I kept telling myself it would take away some of the pressure of shopping for gifts if we did it that way. I'm glad we did it, our gifts to each other showed more creativity and sincerity than anything we could've bought in a store. I love the house you built."

We were interrupted by Daniel's phone ringing. It was Joe calling, and Daniel turned on the speaker.

"Daniel, I got a call from the lady at the Food Bank. If I find out you volunteered me to be Santa's helper, I'm going to come over and kick your butt," Joe yelled.

"Hey man, I'm sitting here with my wife. Watch your language." Daniel exclaimed.

"I'm sorry. Nicole, how are you doing," Joe humbly asked.

"Hi Joe. I need to apologize to you. Santa's elves bowed out at the last minute, and I needed to make a quick decision. I meant to talk to you before Linda called you. Thank you so much for filling in at the last minute.

Otherwise, the Christmas party would be ruined for the kids," I said, with a sigh.

"No problem, sis, you know I would do anything for you. Are you finished buying all the gifts," Joe asked.

"Yea, pretty much, but we just need to get them all wrapped before the weekend."

"I'm off tomorrow. Elaine and I can come over and help you out. I'd also like to give you a $500 donation in case you have any last-minute things to pick up," he offered.

"Thanks so much, Joe. I think I'll buy gift cards and put them in a card for the parents. I'll see you tomorrow."

Daniel was looking at me, his hands on his hips, and a bewildered look on his face. He questioned, "How did you do that?"

"Do what," I asked.

"You completely charmed him. One minute he's talking about kicking my butt, the next minute he's saying he would do anything for you and offering his doggone checkbook. I think you used that same charm on me."

"I doubt it was the same charm, and apparently, it didn't work. You never offered me your checkbook," I asserted.

"No, but I offered you my heart, and it's worth far more that any amount in my checking account." Daniel responded in an alluring tone.

"Hmmm, talking about laying on the charm! And you better not lick your lips," I challenged.

"Lick my lips? What are you talking about," he asked.

"Whenever you're trying to charm me, you lick your lips, and smile, so your dimples are very visible."

We laughed at each other, as we walked to my car.

"Honey, thanks for lunch, and your beautiful company. I would give you a kiss, but I don't want to risk one of my students seeing it. I'll see you in a few hours," Daniel said, while blowing me a kiss.

"Ok. I'd better give Bill a call. I'll wait until I'm in the car, so you won't witness me using my charm twice in one day," I elegantly said.

The rest of the day flew by, and I accomplished so much. I was busy in the kitchen when I heard Daniel unlock the door.

"It smells good in here. What's for dinner," he asked.

"I'm putting together chili for tomorrow's lunch. I'll put it in the crockpot and let it sit in the refrigerator overnight," I responded.

"I can't wait to try it. It looks like you've been very busy this afternoon."

"Yes, I have. The gifts are organized and ready for wrapping. The party is going to be a lot of fun this year. By the way, Bill is happy to be Santa's helper. He and Cheryl will be here tomorrow to help with the gift wrapping. With six of us working together, we should knock it out quickly. And, the best part is, he matched Joe's donation of $500," I said, with excitement.

"You're an amazing lady. What can I do to help?" Daniel asked.

"You can set the table in the dining room. I picked up dinner at the Hibachi restaurant. There goes the oven timer. Would you take the cake out," I asked.

"This cake looks good! What kind is it, and why are we eating in the dining room instead of the kitchen?"

Daniel asked anxiously.

"It's a strawberry pretzel cake, for dessert tomorrow. We're eating in the dining room because I wanted a candlelight dinner with you. We've been running in so many different directions the last few weeks. I just wanted us to slow down and concentrate on each other. Tonight, is about you and me. Kind of like a date night, at home."

"Awww, I love that idea," he said, with a smile.

We ate dinner and afterwards, sat in the living room listening to music. It was a much needed, relaxing evening. One of my favorite songs, "I Believe in You and Me," by Whitney Houston started to play. We danced and held each other, even after the song ended. After dancing to several more songs, we took a bubble bath, and then laid in bed talking.

I moved closer and hugged him. His body was warm and felt so good next to mine. We made love in a sweet, tender way. Tonight, just seemed so special, and so different. I snuggled into his arms and laid my head on his chest. As I was drifting off to sleep, he wrapped his arms around me. I heard him say he loved me, as I eased into a deep sleep.

Chapter 32

Joe and Elaine arrived first the next morning. I had each family's gifts in separate areas, and the wrapping paper was color coded to each family. I didn't want to make a mistake and give out the wrong gift. They were amazed at how much work Daniel, and I had already done.

Daniel had on his Santa hat, mostly to show off. I was glad I had bought a hat for Joe and Bill as well.

Once Bill and Cheryl arrived, we started making a lot of progress. The smell of chili cooking kept them focused, as they knew they would be fed as soon as they were done. I also made corn pudding and a salad.

As we walked down the hall to the dining room, I heard Daniel tell Joe he couldn't have dessert if he didn't eat his salad. Elaine and I looked at each other and rolled our eyes. Sometimes they acted like little boys. Bill blessed the food, and we all dug in. There was little talk from the guys from that point. Elaine, Cheryl, and I talked about our holiday plans. They were really excited about going to Jamaica. We decided to stagger the schedule so each couple could have some alone time. Daniel and I were going next weekend, and Joe and Elaine would follow a few days later. We wanted to spend New Years at home, so Elaine and Joe would have a week alone. Because of Bill's church responsibilities, he and Cheryl would go down after the New Year. I was looking forward to going back, and having Joe and Elaine show us around.

After eating lunch, the guys went up to Daniel's man cave, and we ladies cleaned up. I was so grateful for all their help. We finally sat down and relaxed. It had been a busy few days.

Bill promised to bring his truck on Saturday to transport the gifts. He, Daniel, and Joe would ride together to the club house. Something told me they were going to decorate the truck and make a grand entrance.

On Saturday, Santa and his helpers had a blast at the party. They acted as excited as the kids. I enjoyed watching them pass out the gifts and play with the kids. While we were cleaning up, I heard Joe tell Linda to be sure to include him next year. I smiled at that.

Afterwards, we all went to Bill's house. He and Joe were so excited, you would think they invented the idea of being Santa's helpers. Daniel kept grinning, so I tried my best to avoid eye contact with him. We talked about having a theme party several times during the year. I loved the idea and couldn't wait to get started on the next party.

Bill mentioned his idea of doing something to integrate women into their men's support group. Elaine, Cheryl, and I suggested he do something for Valentine's Day. It could be a small test group, just to see if it would work. The guys really liked the idea, and we spent the next hour tossing around different ideas. Bill had a good idea which couples he thought would benefit the most, as well as provide valuable input. He asked if Daniel and I would head the meeting, as he felt the couples would be more receptive and interactive to us than they would be to counselors or therapists. We agreed to do it, and Bill ended by saying not to do too much research to prepare. Boy, he knew me very well. It had been a great day, and a perfect ending to the week.

Chapter 33

Nicole and I were having a great time in Jamaica. We enjoyed exploring the area and eating the local food. Once Joe and Elaine arrived, the fun really began. They seemed to know everything about the area. Joe and I went fishing, while Nicole and Elaine went shopping. We brought home enough fish to last a while. Our Christmas dinner had a Jamaican theme. I don't think I've ever eaten so much food.

We also went on a river cruise. It ended up being the same ship we cruised on for Nicole's birthday last year. I was able to enjoy it much more this time. Her giddy five-year-old self was bubbling over with excitement. I noticed Elaine was grinning a lot as well. Joe had taken her on this cruise the day he proposed to her. He had mentioned it to me when I asked for advice about Nicole's birthday surprise. The four of us were walking towards the house as the sun was setting. It was a beautiful view.

Nicole stopped to take pictures, and Elaine remarked that the house seemed to be surrounded by hearts. Joe stopped to hug her. Nicole and I kept walking, to give them their privacy. It really was a beautiful area, and I was glad I didn't sell the house. It didn't have any special meaning to me until the first time I brought Nicole here. Now, I'm looking forward to coming back more often.

A few days later, we said our goodbyes to Elaine and Joe. We really enjoyed the holiday, and spending time with them. As much fun as we had, we were anxious to get back home and bring in the New Year alone. I had a feeling Joe and Elaine wouldn't miss us too much. They were acting like teenagers and seemed to be lost in their own little world. I thought it was cute, and totally understood that feeling.

It was New Year's Eve, and the sunrise was beautiful. Nicole was hogging the bed, as usual, and I woke up close to the edge. I watched her while she slept. She was a beautiful lady, sleeping, or awake. She must be having a great dream, she kept smiling in her sleep. I sure hope that dream was about me. I eased out of bed, trying hard not to disturb her rest. I thought she would enjoy breakfast in bed this morning.

She was yawning and stretching when I returned to check on her.

"Good morning sleeping beauty," I said, seductively.

She smiled, and I turned to mush. I don't think I've ever loved her as much as I do at this moment. While she was in the bathroom, I went back to the kitchen to get breakfast. I found a new brand of tea in Jamaica that I thought she would like, and it seemed to be a hit with her. I turned the music on, and we enjoyed our last break-fast of the year. I suggested we go for a run later, and she thought that was a good idea.

She followed me as I took the tray back to the kitchen. We washed the dishes and put them away. I noticed her looking at me and wondered what was on her mind.

"Daniel, there is something about you in a sleeveless t-shirt that completely turns me on. You are a sexy man," Nicole said, in a flirtatious way.

I licked my lips and smiled at her.

"Really? Let's go take a shower together. I've been working hard at the gym, and I'll show you my six pack," I said, smiling, and making sure she saw my dimples.

"You are such a tease," she scolded.

I leaned down to give her a kiss. She kept looking at me, so I flexed my muscles on purpose. I think we both needed that shower to cool us off.

"Let's change things just a little bit," she said, while trying to recover her composure. "Why don't we take the Christmas tree down, then go for a run. That way, we can enjoy a shower together afterwards, and have the rest of the day to relax and get ready for our gift exchange. I'll make you whatever you want for dinner."

"That's fine with me. Will you make banana pudding for me," I asked, in a boyish manner.

"Of course. What else would you like?"

"Macaroni and cheese, collard greens, and baked chicken," I said.

"Ok, I'll need to run to the store to pick up a few things. Why don't you come with me."

It was a busy day, and we accomplished all our goals. Now it was time to relax and have our gift exchange. Nicole asked that I put on a sweater so that she wouldn't be distracted, and, after laughing, I agreed. I'll show her my muscles later.

She had an envelope and a wrapped gift in her hand. She gave me the envelope first. I opened it and began reading her note.

"Daniel, this has been an incredible year. I don't know where to begin. It has been a year filled with love, fun, and wonderful surprises. Did I mention love? It has been 365 days of you loving me and showing me how special I am to you. I feel like I love you more every day. My heart is overflowing. Thank you for loving me the way that you do."

I opened the box she handed me. Inside was the deed to the house. It had been changed to include my name. She said she wanted to make sure I knew this was my home too. I smiled and gave her a big hug.

"Thank you honey. Loving you is the easiest thing I've ever done. You will always be #1 in my life, and in my heart," I said, with a smile.

Now it was my turn. I handed her a heart shaped envelope.

"Nicole, you hold the key to my heart, and I think you already know that. This year has been filled with so many highlights. When I look back, it's hard to choose my

favorite one. I never knew it was possible to be loved as much as you love and take care of me. If I had to choose my favorite day this year, I think I would choose the day you became my wife, and my life partner. Please hold on to my hand, and never let go."

Her eyes were filling with tears, but I wasn't through yet. I gave her a small box. Inside was a key, dangling from a heart-shaped chain. The words #Team Washington were printed on the heart. Tears were rolling down her face. I wiped them away and handed her one more box. Inside was the deed to the house in Jamaica. I had added her name to the deed. The tears were really flowing, and I knew there was no need for words. I took her in my arms, and I held her.

Later, we laid in bed listening to music and talking. Finally, it was 11:55.

"Honey, you know the new year can't begin without me giving you the song I chose for us. My tribute to us for the new year is a song by Al Jarreau called "We're in This Love Together." We ended the year and began the new year making love, as Al sang his song.

A few hours later, I heard Nicole in the bathroom. When she returned to bed, I scooted closer to her and wrapped her in my arms.

"Happy New Year, Honey," I said.

"Happy New Year to you too. Getting a hug from you is the best way to start the year. I thought you were upset with me when I woke up and saw you close to the edge of the bed," she said, close to tears.

I wasn't about to get into that conversation at three in the morning.

"Honey, we're much better than that. If either of us is upset, we'll talk about it," I reassured her.

I kissed her on the neck, and we both went back to sleep.

♡

Chapter 34

January seemed to have wings, as the days flew by. Our attorney and accountant advised us on the best ways to handle the large sum of money which would come from the settlement from Charles. Since the money would be primarily used for charitable causes, we set up an LLC and decided to open a bank account in a different bank. It was our preference that our names weren't attached to the donations we would be making. The money was finally transferred in the third week of January. It was a relief to have that behind us. Other than Joe, Elaine, Bill, and Cheryl, no one else knew about the money. We knew the first donation would be to our church.

Since February was the month of love, we started the month by having a date night. It was a much needed, and enjoyable evening. It was a cold night, so I turned on the fireplace as soon as we returned home. I turned on the music, and we danced together. I was in a very romantic mood. I also had what I hoped would be good news. I was waiting until the timing was perfect.

We sat down, I wrapped my arms around Nicole, and she leaned her head on my shoulder.

"Daniel, you seem distracted. What are you thinking about," she asked.

"I was just thinking of Valentine's Day and also your birthday. I wanted to run something by you."

"You mean, you're not going to surprise me," she asked.

"It will be a bit of a surprise, but I need to get your input first," I countered.

She looked baffled. I kissed her on the forehead, and thought I'd better tell her before her mind started to wander.

"Bill told me the mountain cabin where we spent our honeymoon is going on the market in two weeks. The guy who owns it also has a house in Florida and has decided to move there permanently. The winters in the mountains are beginning to be too much for him. I was wondering if you think it would be a good idea for us to buy it," I asked, with hope.

I don't believe I've ever seen her speechless before.

"Honey, please tell me your thoughts."

"I think it's a great idea," she gushed.

"I was hoping you would say that. I made enough from the sale of my house to pay cash for it. I'll call him tomorrow, and we can both speak with him. Bill says he has already signed papers with a realtor to list it. Maybe you can call your realtor friend, Katelyn. She was so help-ful with the sale of Joe's home, and mine as well."

"Wow, this is a great surprise," she said, still in a state of shock.

"I'm so glad you feel that way. It goes on the market February 14, which could be our Valentine gift to each other. If it works in our favor, we can close sometime in March, and have it furnished and ready in time to spend your birthday there."

"I sure hope it all works out for us," she said, "my fin-gers are crossed."

"Me too. We'll still have the house in Jamaica. The rental income has been great, and it will be paid off in a few more months. If you want to spend more time there, we can limit the number of rentals. With the cabin, it's close enough for us to have weekend get-aways."

"I'm so excited!" The giddy five-year-old in her was clearly visible.

"That reminds me, the support group's Valentine pro-gram is next weekend. I have an idea, and I'd like to get your thoughts on it," I said, trying to bring us back to reality for the moment.

She was all ears, as she listened intently to my thoughts. Of course, she had several great ideas as well. This was going to be a wonderful support meeting.

Chapter 35

We arrived at the church early Saturday morning and found Bill and Joe enjoying a cup of coffee. I joined them, and Nicole had a cup of tea. They had snacks and drinks in the kitchen, and decided they would bring them out when we had breaks. That would help eliminate distractions during the meeting.

"Joe and I were just saying how much we're looking forward to this program. I'm hoping it will be the first of many. One of us will be with you this morning. Elaine and Cheryl will be here this afternoon, and we'll all become a part of the group. There will be four couples. All of them need some type of intervention. There is one couple who have worked very hard on their marriage. I think they have a good chance of working out their differences and staying together. Work your magic, I know we will all learn a lot from you two," Bill said.

Everyone arrived an hour later. As I gazed around, I

noticed some of the guys looked like they would rather be anywhere else than in this room. We had our work cut out for us.

Bill stood up and started us off with a prayer, then a little history about the group. "As you know, the men's support group was started years ago. It has been a great success. A few months ago, we talked about having events in which we would add women. The addition won't replace the support group. We still feel there are times when men need to get together and talk. You are our test group today, and I'm expecting participation and input from all of you. Now, I'll hand things over to Joe, who is one of the co-founders of the group."

"Good morning, everyone, and thank you for being with us today. I'd like to introduce you to my best friend, Daniel, and his better half, Nicole. Daniel and I have been friends since college. Everyone thinks we're brothers, and they also think I'm the cute one," Joe joked.

There was laughter from the group, which was a good sign.

"Bill and I are so happy he and Nicole are helping us today. Please show Daniel and Nicole some love!"

"Good morning," I said, "and just for the record, no one ever thought Joe was the cute one. Nicole and I are excited to be here today. I would like to start by saying we are not here as experts or advisors. Our hope is that what we share will be helpful, and we hope to learn from all of you as well. Also, this is not practiced or rehearsed, so if I ever have a deer in the headlights look, please bear with me. Nicole will start us off. Pay attention, there will probably be a test. She gives me tests all the time. She calls it a honey-do list, but it's a test just the same."

More laughter, the group was beginning to loosen up. I gave Nicole a fist bump and let her have the reins.

"Good morning," Nicole said, "Before we get started, I need all of the guys to help me change the setup of the room. We won't be needing the tables, so let's push them against the wall. I'd like the chairs in a circle, as if there is a bonfire in the middle. Put a little space between each couple and angle the chairs so that you can look up at each other."

We all did as we were told, and not a single person complained.

"Now, doesn't this feel cozy? It's three days before Valentines, so let's start setting the mood. Thank you all for your help. Now that the guys are awake, and had their morning workout, I would like for the ladies to stand. Reach out your right hand and take your husband's left hand. Guys don't let go of her hand as you stand. We're going to start with a thirty second hug. Wrap your arms around each other, and Joe will start the timer. You must hug the whole time," Nicole directed.

I held her in my arms, and really didn't want to let go when the timer went off. As we sat down, I noticed some of the tension leaving the other couples. They were also looking at each other more.

"A hug cures so many things," Nicole began. "The reason for this experiment is something I learned from Daniel early in our relationship. Many times, we ladies will tell you guys what we want from you, but we don't always ask what you want from us. The first time Daniel told me he wanted me to give him a hug, I was really caught off guard. We're always hugging, and until that moment, I didn't realize he was the one who always started it. A hug is very simple, and sometimes it really does matter who initiates it. Daniel, I know you'd like to share your thoughts about hugs."

"As men," Daniel began, "we're conditioned to be the anchor, shoulder to lean on, problem solver, and many other things. One day Nicole was very upset, and I had no idea why. That didn't stop me from trying to fix it. Nicole is a person who goes completely inward when she is upset. She needs to analyze everything. She is not a person who rants and raves, and there is no getting her to talk about her feelings until she's ready. That day I learned how important it is to really know your partner. We had only been seeing each other a few months, and that was the moment when I realized I was in love with her, and that I would do anything to keep her happy. All I knew was that I never wanted to see her so upset, and I needed to fix it. Since I wasn't getting any help from her, I had no idea what I was fixing. On an impulse, I pulled her in my arms and held her. I was not about to let go, and after a few minutes, she wrapped her arms around my waist, and I knew I was making progress. Sometimes, when you don't know what to do or say, just hold her in your arms."

One of the guys raised his hand and began to speak.

"My wife is a lot like that. When I try to help, we usually end up having an argument which is a lot worse than the original problem. It seems like you two have worked that out. What is your secret," he asked.

"No secret, really," I said. "Sometimes it's easier to get results if you're talking about things when you're not in the middle of the problem. Both of you are way too emotional and stubborn if you're trying to solve issues at that time. Nicole and I aren't TV watchers, so we listen to music and talk every night. One night we talked about what we needed from each other. I told her there was nothing wrong with the way she solved problems, but I was asking that she not shut me out or close the door in my face. We agreed that if she was upset and not ready to talk about it, she would tell me that, and I would give her space. The good thing is, we've not had that issue again. Over time, and with a lot of hard work, our communication has become so much better."

"That sounds like a good idea. I'm going to try it," he said.

"Don't tell me, tell your lady," I urged.

He turned to his wife and began talking. We couldn't hear what he was saying, which was perfectly ok. The smile on her face told us everything we needed to know. It was a good time to take a break. Joe's timing was perfect, as he entered the room with drinks and snacks.

Fifteen minutes later, the ladies had not returned. I decided to move forward.

"I never could understand why ladies take so long in the bathroom. I'll bet they're in there talking about us. Let's send them a text and see how fast they come back. Make it a romantic one and notice how they look at us when they return," I challenged the group.

Little did I know, Nicole was in the bathroom telling the ladies something similar, and they beat us to it. Suddenly, our phones started buzzing at the same time. I looked around the room at the other guys, and we all had goofy grins on our faces.

The rest of the morning went very well. I was surprised at the honesty and openness of them all. The guys doing most of the talking were the same ones who, in the beginning, looked like they were forced to come. It was almost lunch, and of course, Joe had to stir things up.

"My wife will be here this afternoon, so I want to get this out before she comes. What do you do when your wife hogs the bed every night," Joe asked.

Nicole and I looked at each other. I noticed she had an amused look on her face.

"I think I'll be in trouble, no matter how I answer this, so I'm going to turn it over to Nicole. Honey, tell them what you tell me when I complain that you're hogging 3/4 of the bed," I urged.

"I tell you that I'm just trying to hug you in my sleep, and you keep moving," she said, with an innocent smile.

"Do you see how sweet and angelic she looks when she says that? How can I argue with that? Brothers, choose your battles. Some nights I sleep with my arms wrapped around her. In the beginning, she thought I was being romantic, but truthfully, I was trying to prevent falling over the edge." I followed her response.

Everyone laughed at that. Nicole gave me the biggest smile.

"Let's head to the dining room to eat," I said.

The first two hours after lunch went extremely well. We talked about finances, children, dealing with exes, and many other things. Everyone got in on the conversations. We had one more hour left, and one of the guys raised his hand and asked to speak.

"I just wanted to thank you for all you taught us today. Two weeks ago, my wife asked me for a divorce. She said she would be willing to work on our marriage if I came here today. I must admit, I felt she was telling me what to do, and I almost didn't come. Then I realized that I didn't want to live without her, so I pushed my male ego to the side, and here I am. I especially want to thank you, Nicole, for starting the day with the thirty-second hug. I was wondering what first step to take to get close to my wife again. It was difficult at first, but it made a big difference in our day. I didn't want to end the hug when the timer went off. Daniel, you're the man! I noticed the way your wife looks at you when she doesn't know anyone is watching. My goal is to have my wife look at me that way too," he admitted.

He took his wife's hand in his and looked in her eyes.

"Baby, this is our chance to start a new and better beginning. I love you and want to spend the rest of my life with you by my side. Please give us a second chance," he pleaded.

She agreed, and this started a chain reaction. Each man got up and made a declaration of love to his wife. We were all getting emotional, and Nicole said this was a good time for a hug. We took our wives in our arms and held them tightly.

It was safe to say the day had been successful. One of the ladies raised her hand. I was hoping this didn't set off more emotion.

"Our family owns a restaurant, and we would like to invite all of you for dinner tonight, our treat. I know it's the last minute, but it's our way of continuing the good vibes for a little longer today. Please say you'll come," she asked.

We all agreed.

"Before we end the day, Nicole and I have a Valentine card for each of you. Inside is an invitation for a one week stay at our home in Jamaica. Just a warning, the house has magical powers. You won't leave without falling madly in love with each other. We hope you enjoy your visit," I said, taking Nicole's hand, and ending the day on a good note.

Chapter 36

I woke up Valentine's morning and reached out to hug Nicole. Her side of the bed was empty, so I went looking for her. I walked down the hall and could hear her singing in the kitchen. She was making breakfast.

"Good morning, Honey, you beat me to it. I was going to cook breakfast for you this morning. This is the day of love, and I plan to pamper you," I said, and gave her a kiss.

"You pamper me every day. Today, let's share the pampering. By the way, Elaine and I have scheduled massages for all of us this afternoon," she said.

"That sounds great. I'll look forward to that. Joe and I are taking the two of you out to dinner. It's a Japanese restaurant where they cook right at your table."

"Oh, I've been to one of those restaurants before. It's neat. I think you will enjoy it," she said.

"I keep forgetting to tell you, Bill said Cheryl wants to know the name of your face cream."

"What do you mean," she asked.

"She told Bill it makes your skin look glow-y. I have no idea what that means, I'm just repeating what he said."

"Oh, ok, I'll give you the name of it," Nicole said.

"Can you just call her and give it to her," I asked.

"No, I'll let you tell Bill. Here's a pen and piece of paper, so you can write the name down. Are you ready?" Nicole sounded excited to share.

"Sure, go ahead," I said.

"Now, it's all capital letters. The name is DANIEL," she said.

"Huh," I asked, confused.

"There is no special cream. Daniel, you are the reason for the glow on my face," Nicole professed.

"Honey, that is so sweet. You made my day." I gave her a hug.

"I love you, sweetheart, and I thank you for making me so happy. Come on, let's eat before our breakfast gets cold," she ordered.

After breakfast, we went separate ways to knock out some errands. Afterwards, we went to Katelyn's office to sign documents to put an offer on the mountain cabin. We could have done it electronically, but Nicole had a beautiful Valentine basket for Katelyn, and wanted to deliver it in person. Katelyn said the listing agent told her the seller would likely make a decision tomorrow or the next day. Knowing that was helpful. That way, we wouldn't keep looking at our phones all day.

Now, it was time for our massages. Joe and Elaine were in the room next to ours. I don't think I've ever been so relaxed. I fell asleep soon after the massage started. I woke up when the masseuse turned my head, to work on my neck and shoulders. Nicole was facing me, and puckered her lips, as if she was sending a kiss my way. I couldn't help but to smile. She made this day so special for me.

We all got dressed, and sat in the lobby eating oranges, and drinking lots of water. They had a Valentine special, which Joe and I signed up for. It would allow us to get two monthly couple massages for the next year. Feeling this good was worth every penny I spent on the special.

When Nicole and I got home, I set the alarm clock, and we took a nap.

We all met at the restaurant a few hours later. The inside was set up very well. There were sections for different sized groups, and we were lucky to get an area for four and didn't have to eat with strangers. It was fun watching the cook set up and cook everything right in front of us. The food was good too.

"Joe, this place is nice, how did you find it," I asked.

"One of the medical students told me about it. I like that it's off the beaten path, affordable, and the food is great. We'll have to bring Bill and Cheryl with us next time," Joe replied.

"Sounds good, they will love it. Let's wait for Elaine and Nicole at the front. It's getting crowded, and I don't want to take up anyone else's space," I suggested.

"True, and there's no telling how long they will be in the bathroom. I can never understand why women spend so much time in public bathrooms," Joe rhetorically questioned.

"I'm sure they're in there talking about us and comparing notes. What are you doing later this evening," I asked.

"Elaine wants to go to the movies, what about you two?" Joe asked.

"Just going home to relax. Nicole has been pampering me all day, now it's my turn to pamper her. Here they come, and it looks like they have met some new friends. Let's get them out of here before they find another reason to keep talking," I said.

We made it home, and while Nicole was changing clothes, I turned on the music, turned down the lights, and turned the fireplace on. The ambiance was perfect. I bought her a single red rose earlier and hid it in the pantry. Luckily, she was looking at her phone when I came out of the kitchen. I was standing in front of her when she put the phone down. As she looked up at me, I took the rose from behind my back, and kneeled in front of her.

"Happy Valentine's Day to the love of my life," I said seductively.

She gave me a big smile; I pulled her closer and kissed her. At that moment, my phone buzzed.

"I'm sorry Honey, I'm expecting an important text. I promise I'll turn the phone off as soon as I answer this," I said.

After responding to the text, I asked her to dance with me. Our favorite Jeffrey Osborne song, "We Both Deserve Each Other's Love," was playing, and I started singing to her. Now, I know I don't sound as good as Jeffrey does, but I don't think she cared. When the song was over, we sat on the sofa, and I wrapped my arms around her.

"Honey, I'm so lucky to have you in my life," I said.

"It's not luck, Daniel, we work really hard on our relationship. I love what we have together," she replied.

"True. I've enjoyed seeing us both evolve and grow together. I hope you know there is nothing I wouldn't do for you. I have one more Valentine surprise for you. I'll be right back," I said, as I ran out of the room.

I came back into the room and handed her a box.

"Wow, thank you. The paper is so pretty. You did a good job of wrapping it too," she muttered, turning the box in several different angles.

She was driving me crazy with her analyzing, but I managed to keep my cool. Finally, she opened it. Inside was a framed picture of the mountain cabin. A note taped to the frame said *"Home is wherever you are. #Team Washington."*

It took her a moment to figure it out, and when she did, tears formed in her eyes. She turned to me and said, "Does this mean what I think it does?"

"It depends on what you're thinking," I responded.

"Did our offer on the house get accepted?" Nicole asked.

"Yes, the text I received was from Katelyn. I asked her to tell me first so I could surprise you. The picture is one you took when we were there last year. I was hoping for the best, so I had it framed last week. Katelyn did a great job on our behalf. I'm passing her business cards all over the campus. She is amazing."

"Yes, she is amazing, and so are you. I know you also worked hard to make this happen. Thank you," she gushed.

"I know it was originally my idea, but when I saw how excited you were, I knew it was meant for us."

"I don't think I acted overly excited," she remarked.

"Not outwardly, no. The Mama Bear part of you that is so protective of me was acting calm, in case we didn't get it, and you felt you would need to console me," I remarked.

"I guess you really know me well."

"Honey, we're a team. We look out for each other," I reminded her.

"Does that mean you're the team captain?" she asked.

"I think it's a role that is interchangeable with us. That cabin means so much to both of us. I can't wait to go back. Katelyn said she will start setting up inspections tomorrow," I added.

"She's doing a lot of traveling for us. Now I'm glad I put a gas gift card in her Valentine basket. She'll be putting in a lot of miles on her car."

" Honey, you're so thoughtful."

"By the way," she said, "you always talk about me acting like a Mama Bear. Well, you're also very protective. You're like a lion protecting his lioness."

"Yes, and you can always count on that. However, everyone knows the lion needs the lioness to help him survive. I'll always need you by my side, too. Are you ready to call it a night?"

"Aye, Aye, Captain," she said, with a salute.

"You're so cute. Can I lure you up to my place tonight?" I asked flirting a little.

"Of course, lead the way," she answered seductively.

Chapter 37

The court proceedings for Charles and Carolyn were originally scheduled for the end of the month, but I received a call from our attorney saying they had both entered a plea bargain. Carolyn would basically get a slap on the wrist, since the gun she pulled on Nicole was unloaded. She received a five-year sentence, which was reduced to one year, for good behavior. She would be free in a few more months. Charles received ten years for attempted murder. Our attorney asked if we wanted to contest it, but we agreed to let it be, and get them out of our lives. I did ask to place a restraining order against Carolyn, and our attorney agreed to help us with that. In the end, the restraining order would help her as much as it would help us. I really believe if she ran into Nicole again, it would not be a pretty sight.

The inspections on the cabin went very well. There were a few minor issues, which I could easily fix myself.

This may be my chance to give Nicole a honey-do list.

It was closing day at last. We went furniture shopping on our visits to the area for inspections. We decided we would start with our bedroom, the guest bedroom, and the living room. We could take our time with the rest of the house. My one indulgence was buying a king-sized bed. I figured it would take Nicole a while to hog that much space. The furniture was scheduled to be delivered in a few days. Since we wanted to spend the first night in the house, Nicole packed blankets and sleeping bags so we would be comfortable. I didn't tell her that Katelyn and the listing agent worked together, and the furniture was being delivered this morning.

We invited Katelyn and her husband, Mike, to brunch, while waiting for the deed to be recorded.

"Katelyn," Nicole said, "we are so thankful for all you've done for us. You know how much I love buying cards, and this one seemed so much like you."

Katelyn opened the envelope Nicole had given her, and immediately became emotional while reading the card. Mike wiped the tears that started to flow. We had given them an invitation for a one week stay in our home in Jamaica.

"I'm sorry for getting so emotional. This is just perfect, and we thank you so much. Our fifth wedding anniversary is coming up, and we've been looking for the perfect getaway. We never had a honeymoon and were determined to do something big this year. You have no idea how much this means to us," Katelyn, said, as her tears flowed.

"You're so welcome. I know you will enjoy our little piece of paradise," Nicole said, close to tears as well.

At that moment, Katelyn's phone buzzed. She smiled and told us the house was ours. We paid the bill, while Katelyn and Nicole went to the ladies' room. Mike and I knew it would take a while, so we sat at the front of the restaurant talking.

"Daniel, thanks again for your generous gift," Mike said. "What Katelyn didn't tell you was that we just found out we're going to be parents in seven months. Going on this trip means so much to us now."

"Wow, that's awesome. I'll give you my contact with the management company, so you can get the trip scheduled as soon as possible. Let us know if you need an extra set of grandparents," I said, as we shook hands.

Chapter 38

We pulled into the driveway of our new home and sat for a moment to enjoy the view. Other than the birds chirping, there was complete silence. I looked at Nicole and had a feeling we would be spending a lot of time here.

We held hands as we walked to the front door. I scooped her in my arms as I pushed the door open. I wanted to carry her over the threshold of our first home together. She was so excited, and I couldn't wait for her to see the furniture in place.

"Wow! Daniel, this is beautiful. The furniture is exactly where I wanted it. I thought they said they couldn't deliver it for a few more days," she said, with surprise.

"That is true, but I found out the listing agent is related to the guy who owns the furniture store. She and Katelyn worked together to get it delivered today while we were at the closing. When you were telling me where you would place everything, I made a diagram, and left it in the kitchen for the movers," I responded.

"You are so awesome. I thought you were just taking notes on things you needed to do around the house."

"Let's go see the bedroom," I prompted.

I pushed a button on the wall, and music began to play. I took her in my arms and began to dance. After a few dances, we sat on the chaise. At that moment, she noticed the bed.

"That bed looks bigger than the one we saw in the store," she gasped, wide-eyed.

I was having a hard time holding in my laughter. I said, "It's a King size bed. I thought you might need a little more room while sleeping."

She looked at me, and we both started laughing.

We got so much accomplished in only a few hours. I will never again tease her about being over organized, over analyzing, or over researching everything. She had packed everything in the car that we needed for the two nights we would be spending here. It was very chilly, and I was thankful she had packed extra blankets. She also had packed supplies, so that, if we came up here on a whim, we would have the basic things we needed. She had researched the area and found several stores within two miles of the house. We went shopping for food, bottled water, and king size sheets for our bed. I also set up a new alarm system, with cameras. Thankfully, she had also packed my toolbox. The house was beginning to feel like home.

Later that night, we laid in bed talking.

"Daniel, thank you so much for buying this house. I feel like we're on our honeymoon again."

"I feel the same way, honey. Until today, I didn't realize how much I loved this house. You have done a great job of turning it into a home. It has our vibe already," I complimented her.

I pulled her in my arms and kissed her. I slowly made my way down her body. We were both getting aroused. I took her right breast in my mouth as I began licking and sucking on it. I heard her sudden intake of breath, so I let go, and did the same with the left breast. Meanwhile, we let our hands roam up and down each other's bodies. I looked in her eyes, and I'm sure the passion I saw on her face was a mirror image of my face. She climbed on top of me and took over. I started moaning and calling her name. She gave me a sensuous kiss, as we moved together in slow motion. I was having a hard time controlling myself, but I let her have her way with me. She grabbed my hips, pulling me closer to her. When she began to moan and move faster, I rolled her over, and I took control. I slowly moved in and out of her. Finally, we both let loose, and exploded with love for each other. I pulled her in my arms, and I held her. My body was craving her body, and I didn't want to let her go. We held each other as we fell into a deep sleep.

Chapter 39

𝓘n the last few weeks, I've gotten several calls from Charles' attorney. He told me Charles was being transferred to another facility and wanted to talk with me. I had no idea what he could possibly want to talk about, so I put him off for several reasons. For one, I wasn't going to do anything to interrupt Nicole and I as we went through the process of buying the cabin. Secondly, he needed to know I wasn't going to jump just because he summoned me. He needed to put his ego aside and get over the power and control he thought he had. I don't usually keep things from Nicole, but I thought it best not to mention this meeting. I talked with Joe about it, and he offered to come with me. We joked that he was coming along in case I punched Charles and needed bail money. I was hoping it didn't come to that, but I also wasn't taking any crap from him.

I sat across from Charles and waited for him to speak. Suddenly, he seemed very timid.

"Thank you for coming today. I wanted to apologize for the incident in the park, and the mess I've made of your lives," Charles said, with conceit.

"First of all, you could have sent the apology through your attorney. We didn't need to meet for that. Also, my wife and I are doing fine. Your actions had little effect on our lives," I said, matching his smug look.

He visibly cringed when I called Nicole my wife, so I thought I would keep reminding him of that fact.

"If that's all you wanted, we can end this conversation," I said, as I stood up.

"Please, hear me out. I also wanted to thank you for taking such good care of Nicole."

"Charles, my wife and I are a duet, not a threesome. Your thoughts and concerns are of no importance to us. You had your chance, and you blew it. You crumbled her up like a worn-out piece of paper and tossed her aside. You ripped her life apart and left her to pick up the broken pieces by herself." I could feel myself getting angry and had to remember where I was.

"Are you trying to take credit for rescuing her," he asked smugly.

"Not at all. Nicole never needed rescuing, she just needed to be loved. She turned her life around despite all you put her through, and she did it with grace and class. Then I came along and enhanced that turn around. I showed her what it's like to be truly loved and valued, like a real man would do." I couldn't help matching his smugness.

I was enjoying the fact that he was speechless, so I continued to talk, "One last thing, I told you once what I would do to you if I caught you trying to hit on my wife. It still applies. There is no need for any more communication between us. The next time you contact Nicole, I'm going to kick your ass."

"Are you threatening me," he asked in surprise.

"Not a threat, consider it a promise." I lowered my voice and glared at him.

"I think I'll call the guard over and let him know you're threatening me. It's his job to protect me." he said, in a wimpy, cowardly way.

"Help yourself, see how far it gets you," I challenged.

He signaled for the guard to come over. As the guard approached, I turned around at the sound of his voice, and recognized him as one of the guys in our Valentine support group meeting. He immediately recognized me as well.

"Daniel, how are you doing, and how is Nicole," he asked, as we shook hands.

"She's doing great, keeping me busy with her honey-do lists," I replied, trying to hold in my laughter.

Charles looked like he was about to faint, and I was enjoying every minute of his uneasiness.

"Hey man, thanks again for the invitation to stay at your home in Jamaica. We've booked it for May, which is our anniversary. I'm going to ask my wife to marry me again," the guard said.

"That's awesome! That was where I proposed to Nicole. Let me know if you need help finding things to do there." I knew the small talk was adding to Charles' anxiety, and I was enjoying it.

"I apologize for getting off track. Maxwell, was there a reason you called me over here?" the guard asked.

"No, never mind," Charles murmured.

I prepared to leave, and decided to plunge the knife in, and turn it. With a sly grin, I said, "By the way, guard, take care of Mr. Maxwell, he's Nicole's ex."

I turned and walked across the room. Joe stood up as I walked through the lobby door.

"Hey brother, I was beginning to worry. How did it go," Joe asked.

"Let's go to lunch, and I'll fill you in."

We went to The Burger Barn, and I filled him in while we waited for our food.

"That guy is really crazy. I've never seen anyone so arrogant," Joe said, in amazement.

"Well, he better get the message. I'm not playing his stupid games. My favorite part was when he was going to report me to the guard, who ended up being someone I know. It was hard for me to keep a straight face," I laughed.

" Daniel, it always amazes me how many people you know in this town." Joe said, having a hard time hiding his amazement.

"Yeah, and it really comes in handy at times like today. Since our wives are volunteering all day, why don't we take them out to dinner?"

"Great idea! I've been meaning to ask you how you feel about the two of them going to the mountains this week without us," Joe asked.

"I never thought twice about it, Joe. Nicole said they're going to put a woman's touch on our cabin."

"I don't know about you, but I don't want to spend three nights alone," he said.

"So, what do you suggest we do?" I asked.

"I think we should crash their girls' getaway, Daniel. I'm not quite sure how to do that though."

"I'll bring my tool kit, knock on the door, and let them know I'm good with a hammer," I offered.

"That's really corny, Daniel."

"Really? Well, that's the same line I used on Nicole to get her phone number the first time I met her. It worked."

"Right, it was probably your dimples that got her attention." Joe added as a reminder.

We both enjoyed a good laugh, and the waitress showed up with our food.

Chapter 40

It was difficult, but Joe and I made it through two nights without our wives. It was Friday at last, and we were headed to see them. Nicole sent her usual morning text and told me how much she and Elaine had gotten done in the last few days. She promised to send pictures tomorrow before they left to return home. It will be quite a surprise to them when Joe and I show up.

We left early enough to avoid most of the morning rush hour traffic and were making great progress. Only a little over an hour, and we would be there. My phone buzzed, and it was Nicole. That made me a little nervous.

"Hi honey, are you ok?" I asked.

"Yes. I just wanted to tell you that I love you," she softly replied.

"Ahhh, honey, I love you too. What plans do you and Elaine have for today?"

"Just doing some last-minute shopping. We found a

great consignment store yesterday. They got a new shipment in today, so we're going back. What are you and Joe up to?" Nicole asked.

"We're going to breakfast, then do a little work around our houses. Maybe we'll go for a run later today. Do you know what time you're leaving tomorrow?"

"We'll probably leave around 10," she said.

"Great, that should get you home around noon. We'll take you two out to lunch. If you want, I'll schedule a massage for you," I offered.

"That sounds good, but since tomorrow is Saturday, it will probably be a busy day for them. We can do the massage next week."

"You don't have to wait till next week. I'll give you a massage," I said.

"I love that idea even better. I'll look forward to it. Enjoy your breakfast. I love you."

"I love you more, honey. I'll talk with you later today."

I hung up and saw Joe smiling at me.

"Daniel, I know I tease you a lot about being mushy, but I am so glad that you have Nicole in your life. She's good for you, and I've never seen you so happy." Joe said with excitement in his eyes.

"I'm very much in love with her. The best thing is that she knows exactly how I feel about her, and she never takes advantage of me. It feels good to be with someone I can be completely vulnerable with, and still feel completely safe. She is my safety net, and I am hers."

"That is very rare," Joe replied.

"I know. She makes me want to be the best I can be.

There is nothing I would deny her. If she asked for the moon, I would try to find a way to get it for her."

Joe nodded and said, "I think that feeling is mutual. You make her extremely happy, too. She always has a big smile on her face."

"Joe, I'm going to share some things about Nicole's past with you. She was an orphan and grew up moving from one foster home to another. She learned at an early age not to get attached, and to keep her emotions contained. She was very smart and got a full scholarship to college. She studied to be an architect in undergrad. Since the scholarship was only for four years, she paid for her graduate studies by working nights, and attending school during the day. It took her longer to get the degree, and it was a badge of honor for her."

"Wow," Joe exclaimed.

"Yes, she's a determined lady. She didn't share this with me until we had been together for a few months. She said she wanted to make sure I didn't act like I cared, just because I felt sorry for her. By the time she told me, I was head over heels in love, and there was no turning back. That's why I worked so hard on the house I built for our holiday gift exchange the first Christmas we were together. I wanted her to have her own little girl fantasy that no one could ever take away from her. I woke up in the middle of the night and she wasn't in bed. I found her in the living room sitting in front of the house, smiling like a little kid. She gave me her heart that night, and I knew I was going to do everything I could to protect it. It has been wonderful watching her peel back the layers of her life, as she has begun to trust me, and love me more than I could ever imagine being loved," I shared, with a smile.

Joe, looking like he figured it out responded, "I think that explains why she married that fool, Charles. I'm glad you let him have it, Daniel, and I'm also glad I didn't know this story before now. I probably would've kicked his ass for you."

I nodded at him with a confirming smile and interjected, "Well, that still might happen. He better remember what I told him and leave her alone."

"Thank you for sharing this with me, Daniel. I've always thought you two had a very special relationship. Now I can see how special it truly is. You are a great guy, and I'm glad you've found the love of your life."

"Me too. The only regret I have is that my mom never met her. She would've loved her too." I added.

"Your mom would be very proud of you, and I'm sure she is looking down on you and smiling. She did a wonderful job of raising you by herself and instilling so many great qualities in you. Who knows, maybe she sent Nicole to you at the perfect time in both of your lives," Joe said.

"You may be right about that. Nicole definitely has my mom's sense of serenity and calmness. Look, the sign says we're thirty miles away. I can't wait to see my lady."

Joe, matching my excitement to arrive said, "I second that thought, brother."

We were down the street from the cabin, and I asked Joe not to park too close to the house. I didn't want the ladies to see us on the security cameras. Joe and I called them both at the same time, and Nicole answered first. I asked, "Hey honey, what are you doing?"

"Nothing much, what about you?" Nicole replied.

"I'm working on a surprise for you," I said.

"Daniel, it's not nice to tease me like that."

"You're right, I apologize. I'll give you a hint, ok?"

"Ok," she conceded.

"I want you to walk outside," I said.

Joe and I walked closer to the house. Nicole opened the front door, and she and Elaine ran toward us.

♡
Chapter 41

Nicole decided that, for her birthday, she wanted to have a big party for 100 kids. She had been working with several agencies in the last few months, who could help her accomplish this. Sadly, it wasn't hard to find 100 needy kids, but the flip side was that we would make the day a great one for them. I agreed to build two houses if we could find two children with the same birthday as Nicole. We did find them, and I built a fairy princess house for a girl who was turning six, and a spiderman theme house for a boy who was turning seven. The houses were big enough for them to walk inside. We decorated the inside, and added chairs and a small table, so they could entertain their friends. Joe, Bill, and I delivered them to the parents while the kids were in school. The parents promised to send pictures of the kids playing in their little homes.

The birthday party was on Saturday, and Nicole's birthday was on Monday. We asked each child to give us a wish list, and we chose three things from the list. We had a ball shopping for gifts. A local merchant let us borrow his warehouse space, which worked out perfectly. Another merchant volunteered box lunches for each child. We knew they would be too excited to eat, so we decided to give it to them when they were ready to go home. We played several games with them before setting up the gift stations. As an added surprise, we wrapped the gifts so they could enjoy opening them. A few of the older kids asked for bikes, so we put big bows on them.

The kids made a huge birthday card for Nicole. Each of them had signed it, and the older kids wrote birthday messages. The surprise on her face was priceless.

The party was a lot of fun. It was nice to see the kids have a day when they could enjoy themselves, and just be kids. I was happy Nicole chose this way to celebrate her birthday. I wanted the celebration to continue, and I had my own surprises for her.

After church the next morning, I told Nicole I was taking her on a two-night mini vacation for her birthday. I really wanted to surprise her, but I needed her help packing. I was afraid I would leave something important that she needed, plus, I'm not as organized as she is.

Thankfully, she's getting better at letting me surprise her. She didn't ask where we were going, in fact, shortly after I got on the road, she fell asleep.

A few weeks ago, I ran into Don, one of my former co-workers. When he and his wife retired, they bought a house at the beach. Less than a year later, they decided they weren't ready for retirement, or to make the beach their permanent home. They decided to use the beach house as a vacation rental and moved back to town. Thankfully, the house was free this week. Since I only needed a few days, he waived the rental fee. He showed me pictures of the house, and I couldn't wait for Nicole to see it.

We were almost there when she woke up.

"Sleeping beauty is awake," I said, with a grin.

She smiled, and asked where we were.

"About thirty minutes away. Are you hungry?" I asked.

"A little. I brought some snacks; would you like to stop and eat? You probably need a break anyway," Nicole replied.

"Sure, that's a good idea."

She had placed an insulated bag in the back seat when we got in the car. I wondered what was in it, but knew if I asked, she would start asking questions about where we were going. Turns out the bag was filled with sandwiches, fruit, snacks, and water. She was always prepared!

I pulled over at a rest stop so we could eat and enjoy the beautiful weather. It was a much-needed break. Shortly after, we were at the beach house. The pictures of it were nice, and it was even better in person. We unpacked the car, changed clothes, and went for a walk on the beach. It was a beautiful beach, and not crowded at all.

Later, we found a grocery store and a nice restaurant. Nicole went to the store to get breakfast food for tomorrow, and I went to the restaurant to pick up dinner. We had a relaxing meal and walked on the beach again that evening. The sunset was beautiful, and she took lots of pictures.

We showered together and sat in the living room listening to music. It had been a long day, but surprisingly, we weren't as tired as we expected to be. Being near the ocean was very relaxing.

"Daniel, thank you for bringing me here. This area is beautiful, and the house is very nice too," she said, with little girl gushiness.

I smiled at her. The glow on her face was so beautiful. It was pure luck that I ran into Don, and I was very thankful for his generosity. I sat across from her and held her hands in mine.

I professed my gratitude again as a reminder, "Honey, a year ago, I asked you to marry me. Boy, I had no idea what I was getting into. It has been a year of happiness and incredible love, more than I ever thought possible. Sure, we had some challenges, and we worked through them together. They made us, and the love we share, so much stronger. Thank you for saying yes. I'm so happy to have you by my side, and in my heart."

I stood up and pulled her in my arms. She wrapped her arms around me and hugged me tightly. When we broke apart, I saw so much passion and love on her face. I took her hand and led her down the hall to the bedroom. I said, "Honey, I know your birthday is tomorrow, but I want to give you your gift now."

I reached under the pillow, pulled out a small box, and handed it to her. Her eyes lit up as she opened it. It was a double heart necklace. The hearts were intertwined, just as our hearts are. I placed it around her neck and kissed her.

We laid in bed, kissing, and holding each other. Then, we made love. It was a combination of tender, gentle lovemaking, and wild, hot sex.

I wrapped my body around hers. Neither of us wanted to let go of the other.

Chapter 42

The next morning, I scooted close to Nicole and gave her a big hug. I lovingly said, "Happy Birthday to my favorite little girl, my lovely lady, and the woman I adore."

She turned over and smiled. I detected the giddy five-year-old in her, and it made me smile too.

"Let's have a blueberry muffin and a cup of tea on the beach. We can watch the sunrise, and you can get some great pictures," I said.

"That's a great idea. Also, I bought coffee for you if you'd rather have that." She responded as she was always looking out for me.

We decided to drive the three blocks to the beach. We ate in the car while waiting for the sun to make its appearance. There were several cars in the parking lot. I guess we weren't the only early birds.

We had a beautiful walk along the beach. Once the

sun burst through the clouds, it really began to show off. Nicole took lots of pictures, and we continued our walk. After walking several miles, we stopped to relax. The view was beautiful, and the sound of the water hitting the shore was so relaxing.

We started digging in the sand, and soon we had the beginning of a sandcastle. Imagine a sandcastle built by an architect and an engineer; it looked pretty good. A little girl broke away from her mom and ran toward us.

"That's bootiful! I like your castle. Can I help?" the little girl asked loudly.

Her mother started to protest, but Nicole said we would love to have her help. We had a few moments of silence, while the three of us worked on our castle. The little girl's mother smiled and sat down to watch us.

"Today is my birthday, and my mom said I can do anything I want," the little girl said.

"Wow, today is my birthday too. How old are you," Nicole asked.

She held up four plump little fingers.

"Well, happy birthday to us both. What's your name?"

"My name is Nicole, but my Daddy calls me Nikki. This is my mom, Jennifer. My Dad is in the Air Force. Mom says he's serving our country and can't be here for my birthday," she proudly responded.

"Ahhh, my name is Nicole too. It's nice to meet you, Nikki. This is Daniel. Let's build a big castle to celebrate our birthday." Nicole said with excitement.

We had fun playing in the sand. Jennifer's phone rang, and she told Nikki it was her dad calling. Nikki had a big smile on her face while she talked. When she hung up, she told us her dad said he had a big birthday surprise for her. She couldn't contain her excitement.

"We have to go now, so we're leaving you in charge of the sandcastle. I hope your birthday is the best," I told her.

"Thank you. I'll take good care of the castle. Happy birthday, Ms. Nicole. I hope we see you again," she said, with excitement.

The two birthday girls exchanged hugs. We waved goodbye and walked to our car. It was a very relaxing day. I cooked breakfast, then we took a nap. We decided to have an early dinner and return later for another walk on the beach.

The beach was unusually crowded that evening, and we saw a news truck. I was hoping no one had drowned. As we walked closer to the crowd, I realized we were at the spot where we built our castle earlier today. The castle was still in place, and other buildings had been added. It looked like a village. I heard a little girl talking, and realized it was Nikki, and she was being interviewed by the news reporter.

"Mommy and me were walking this morning and saw a man and lady building a castle. It was so bootiful, and I asked if I could help. They said yes, and we made two buildings. Then, I told them it was my birthday, and the lady said it was her birthday too. Her name is Nicole too, but my Daddy calls me Nikki. They had to leave, and said I was in charge of the castle. Mommy is a nurse, so she made a hospital beside the castle. Then, my Daddy surprised me and came here. He's in the Air Force. He made an airplane and put a flag in front. Daddy said we had to go, and he would put a sign up so nobody would mess with the castle. We came back later and saw more buildings," she gushed.

She was very dramatic and flinging her arms while talking. Nicole and I made our way to the front of the crowd, and Nikki saw us.

"That's my birthday friend!" Nikki shouted, as she ran to Nicole and gave her a hug.

The two of them enjoyed their few moments of fame. The ice cream truck came by and gave them free ice cream. I had a chance to chat with her parents while she was concentrating hard on the ice cream. Her Dad, Timothy, said she wanted to learn big girl words since she was now four. This week's word was "beautiful". Timothy said everything was "bootiful", according to Nikki. He said he would look forward to her new word next week.

The sun was beginning to call it a day, and the crowd slowly began to disperse. Timothy picked Nikki up. She dropped her head on his shoulder and fell asleep. It had been a great day for the birthday girls. We exchanged contact information, and Nicole and I walked home.

We listened to music, as the evening winded down. It had been quite a day of surprises.

"Daniel, I know you didn't plan today, but it seems like something you would do," Nicole said.

"It really was a beautiful day, and I'm sure Nikki's Dad had a lot to do with some of the things that happened. Every time I see the giddy five-year-old in you, I'm going to think of Nikki. She has quite a personality." I said.

Nicole agreed, "Yes, she does. I want to thank you again for the beautiful necklace. I love it."

"You know, the funny thing is, one day I was doing some work on the computer, and an ad for a jewelry store came up. In fact, it was the same store where I bought your wedding ring. I went in the next day, and they had the necklace in the store. I couldn't resist it."

"I absolutely love it." Nicole exclaimed.

"They said I could also put our initials on the hearts, but I thought that would take away from the beauty of the necklace."

"I agree with you on that," she said.

"I have one more surprise for you, Nicole. It will be more of an anniversary gift, rather than a birthday gift. I'm planning a trip to St. Thomas, Virgin Islands, in the fall."

"You're so wonderful. Thank you for making my day special. I love you so much, not because of the things you give me, but because of how thoughtful and loving you are. It will be hard to go back to reality tomorrow." Nicole sighed after her response.

"Let's not think about reality right now. Let's go to bed, and make more memories of this day," I said, with a wink.

Chapter 43

May was just beginning, and already becoming a busy month. Graduation was coming up, and this would be a very special one for me. I decided not to renew my contract, so, in a few weeks, I would be free to do whatever I wanted. I was certain Nicole would make sure I was not too idle.

I always enjoyed being an engineer, and after retiring, I decided to teach. It has been so rewarding. This year was especially fun because I knew it would be my last year. I was hoping that I had made a difference in my students' lives. I really saw the impact I had made when they gave me a retirement party. Most of my students from the last five years came to see me off into the easy life, as they called it.

The biggest surprise came a few days later. I was voted professor of the year. Nicole and Joe did a great job of keeping this a secret. I didn't even know I was being considered for this honor. My students built a fairy princess house for Nikki, Nicole's birthday friend. All of their names were printed on a plaque, which they placed inside, on one of the walls. They had also hung my picture and a picture of my award. I was feeling very emotional when Nikki and her parents walked into the room. She ran toward me and gave me a big hug. The expression on her face was priceless when my students presented the house to her. She was using more of her big girl words, and told us the house was extra, extra bootiful, and she loved it.

After the awards ceremony, we had a nice dinner. Nikki and her parents lived two hours away and left shortly afterwards. I couldn't wait to see pictures of her in her new little home.

Later that evening, I asked Nicole how she managed to arrange the two surprises so perfectly.

"Don't give me too much credit," she said, "two of your students first approached Joe. They wanted you to know how much you meant to all of them and needed help. Joe called me, and we came up with several ideas. The house they built for Nikki was an added plus. Those two students were in your class and helped you build the house for me a few years ago. They talked about how much fun all of you had doing that, and wanted to do something that would always have your mark on it, and make someone else happy, just as you always do. I thought of Nikki and called her parents. They loved the idea and knew Nikki would too."

"Wow! The party and the award were the biggest surprises. Thank you for doing that." I thanked Nicole.

"Daniel, you give so much to others. I'm so happy to see it come back to you. You're always surprising me, and it felt good to surprise you this time." She gave me her million-dollar smile.

I kissed her, and we headed to bed.

"Just think, a few more weeks, and I'm all yours. I'm really going to enjoy my retirement and spending more time together," I said, while hugging her.

"I'm looking forward to it too, but I don't think you will have a lot of free time. The houses you have built are getting a lot of attention. It might be a new career for you." Nicole added before drifting to sleep.

The next week was graduation, and two weeks later I was officially retired forever.

Chapter 44

*I*t was an enjoyable summer. We drove to Maryland and spent three days with Ms. Betsy. She was so excited to see us, but no more excited than we were. I could never forget the part she played in my younger years, and all the love she and her family showed me when my mom passed. She has adapted well to the area and has made several new friends. It was Nicole's idea to visit, and I'm so glad we did.

We went to the mountain cabin several times. It was completely decorated and really felt like home. The weather was much cooler in the mountains than it was at home. We had some very relaxing times there, discovered the local area, and found some great restaurants. We also found several parks and trails. We were having the best time of our lives. Joe and Elaine went to Hawaii for their anniversary and had a great time too.

Finally, it was September, and time for our anniversary

trip to St. Thomas. I only planned one event, and the rest of the week, we were going to be spontaneous. Our first night there, we went on what was called Kon Tiki Party Boat. It took us on a tour of several other Islands. It was loud, and a lot of fun. The best part was that the tour was in the evening. The sunset was amazing. We got great pictures of the sun dipping into the sea.

I woke up the morning of our anniversary and watched Nicole sleeping. She looked so angelic. In the last few months, she was getting much better at not hogging the bed. She claimed she didn't realize how much space she was taking up until I bought the big bed for the cabin. I whispered, "Good morning sleeping beauty." She gave me a smile.

After all this time, her smile still turns me to mush. We had breakfast and explored the island. It was a beautiful place. That evening, we had a candlelight dinner in our hotel room. I couldn't keep my eyes off her.

"Honey, this has been an incredible year. You are the best wife, friend, and lover. Thank you for making me so happy." I said to Nicole.

She smiled and responded, "That certainly goes both ways, Daniel. I look forward to every new day in our lives. Thank you for making me feel so loved and valued. You always put me first, and that means so much."

I agreed while multi-tasking to set the mood, "We are each other's number one priority. Everything and everyone else take second place. I love that about us. I heard a song while you were sleeping that made me think of us, and of our love for each other. It's called "This Will Be

(An Everlasting Love)," by Natalie Cole. It describes our love perfectly. Listen to the words."

The song had an upbeat sound. I took her hand and we danced.

Later that evening, we lay in bed talking. I began undressing her, with my eyes, and with my hands. She smiled at me as I removed each piece of clothing. I took off my clothes and pulled her close to me. We made sweet, tender love to each other. In some ways, it felt like the first time, in some ways it felt better than the first time.

I held her in my arms and kept kissing her. I thought I heard her moaning, and realized it was me. I didn't want to let go of her. We both became aroused and made love again.

I covered her with the sheet and pulled her in my arms. We fell into a sound sleep.

We spent three more days in our own little world, then returned home.

Chapter 45

$\mathcal{I}$t was a beautiful fall day. Elaine and I volunteered at the Food Bank, then picked up lunch at The Burger Barn, and headed to Elaine's house. Daniel and Joe were working out at the gym. They were planning to pick up lunch afterwards and join us. We were starting on dessert when Elaine's phone rang.

"Hi Joe, are you headed home?" she asked.

"Elaine, I have some bad news, and I need you to act calm. Is Nicole with you?"

"Yes," Elaine replied.

"Daniel was in an accident. I don't want either of you to drive, so I'm sending a cop to pick you up. He should be there in about five minutes. I'll give you more details when you get here."

Elaine hung up her phone and looked to me, "Nicole, that was Joe. He's at the hospital and is sending a cop to pick us up."

"Is everything ok?" I asked with confusion.

"I don't know yet, he didn't give me any details."

The doorbell rang, and it was our escort. My mind was twirling, but I tried to remain as calm as possible considering I had so little information. The fact that Daniel didn't call was very frightening. Elaine and I got in the back seat. She reached for my hand, and we prayed together.

Joe was waiting at the front door when we arrived at the hospital. He took us to a private room and delivered the news.

"Nicole, we were a block from the gym. A car ran a red light and hit Daniel's car. I was a few cars behind him and was able to start emergency medical procedures quickly. He's still unconscious. We were able to get some x-rays, and a CT scan. So far everything looks good," Joe stated, in a monotone.

"Is he going to die, Joe?" I asked.

"Honestly, I don't know. Hopefully he will regain consciousness soon. We will know a lot more after that."

"I want to be with him," I insisted.

When we entered Daniel's room, I experienced a feeling of peace and calm. He was slightly elevated in the bed and appeared to be in a deep sleep. I sat beside his bed and held his left hand. Joe and Elaine sat in chairs near the door.

"Daniel, you told me once, to take your hand and never let go. You also told me you wanted me to always be by your side. I'm going to do both things right now," I began, as I held his hand.

I fought back the tears as I massaged his hand. I knew he needed me to be strong at this moment, so I wrapped my hands around his, and tried to send strength and healing rays to him.

"If you're leaving us, I want my voice and my words to be the last thing you hear. On the other hand, if you're making your way back, I want my voice to be the first thing you hear. The words are the same, no matter what happens," I said, hopeful as I could be in this moment.

"Always know that you are loved, and cherished. You are the light of my life. You are the best husband, friend, and life partner I could ever ask for. You are the man of my dreams. I love you with all my heart."

I repeated the words several times, as if I were chanting.

I looked up, and saw a tear roll down his face. I knew this was a good sign, but I was too scared to move. His tears started flowing. Out of the side of my eye, I saw Joe approach the bed. Daniel began to cry out loud.

"Mom, please don't leave me again. Please, please, let me stay with you this time," Daniel cried.

I held his hand tightly and kept telling him how much he was loved. He opened his eyes and kept blinking.

"Nicole? Is that you," he asked.

"Yes, welcome back," I said as my tears began to flow.

"I just had a weird dream. I must tell you about it," he said in a rush.

"You need some rest; you can tell me later," I said.

"No, I need to tell you now, before it fades away, and I forget some of the details. I dreamed I was with my mom. She told me she's always watching over me, and that she is so proud of me. I kept reaching for her hand, but she started pushing me away, and her voice started to fade after she told me she loved me but wasn't ready for me yet. I started to cry, and she massaged my scalp, like she used to do when I was a kid. Then, I heard your voice telling me how much I was loved. The more I heard your voice, the more my mom's voice faded away, until all I could hear was you. Mom's voice was pushing me away, and your voice was bringing me closer." Daniel explained, slightly baffled.

"Honey, are you crying? Why am I in this bed," he asked, with a stunned look.

Things began moving rapidly at this point. His monitors were making noises, someone from the lab came in to take blood, the nurse and doctor came into the room. Shortly after, he was taken to radiology to have an MRI brain scan.

Joe went with him; Elaine and I stayed in the room. It was the longest two hours of my life. Finally, the door opened, and they wheeled the bed back into the room. Daniel's eyes were closed. I knew he was exhausted, so I reached for his hand. He opened his eyes and smiled at me.

Shortly after, the doctor came in to give us the results of all of the tests Daniel had had that day. It was all good news. There didn't appear to be any brain or neurological damage. The bloodwork was good, there were no broken bones, and his heart was in good shape. He was indeed a lucky man. They wanted him to stay overnight for observation. After the doctor left, Joe gave his version of the test results.

"Hey brother, good thing you're so hardheaded. The fact that you're so healthy also worked in your favor. I guess eating all those salads and turkey burgers really helped," Joe smirked.

We all laughed, and it was a welcome relief.

"Do you know what happened to the person who hit me," Daniel asked.

"The last I heard; he was in ICU. I'll check later. Nicole, I know you'll want to stay overnight. Do you want me to take you home to pick up anything?" Joe asked.

"That would be nice, thank you Joe."

Before I could say anything else, Elaine seemed to be reading my mind.

"Don't worry, Nicole, I'll stay here with Daniel while Joe takes you home," she offered.

Daniel had a restful night. I knew he was feeling better the next morning because the first thing he asked upon awakening was how I felt. I assured him I was fine, and that breakfast was on the way. He said he was starving, which was another good sign that he was returning to his normal self. After breakfast, the doctor came in and said Daniel would be discharged later that day. Joe and Elaine returned shortly afterwards. Joe told us the guy who hit Daniel had a heart attack while driving. He didn't have any more details. We held hands and said a prayer for him, and his family.

We heard a loud knock, and the door burst open. There stood Carolyn, Daniel's ex-wife. What in the world was she doing here?

"He's gone," she yelled dramatically.

We all looked at her, wondering what she was talking about.

"Tom, my husband, just died! He was driving the car that hit you yesterday," she exclaimed. She started bawling, then dropped to the floor in a dramatic faint.

About the Author

Writing "And I Held Her" was a product of my overactive imagination, life events, and my many "lives" My studies, and love of English and Psychology played a large part in the formation of the characters that were in the story. My career in radiology technology and real estate were helpful as well. I've traveled many years as a military child and spouse which helped develop my love for traveling and discovering new places. I must not forget to also add my inner five-year old, who loves birthdays, and is forever optimistic, which was the biggest impetus in helping on this journey.

– Sheila Magee

Made in the USA
Columbia, SC
26 November 2023

26753475R10133